THE CRITIC
and Other Stories

THE CRITIC
and Other Stories

MARTIN HUNTER

Cormorant Books

Copyright © 2013 Martin Hunter
This edition copyright © 2013 Cormorant Books Inc.
This is a first edition.

No part of this publication may be reproduced, stored in a retrieval system or transmitted, in any form or by any means, without the prior written consent of the publisher or a licence from The Canadian Copyright Licensing Agency (Access Copyright). For an Access Copyright licence, visit www.accesscopyright.ca or call toll free 1.800.893.5777.

 Canada Council for the Arts / Conseil des Arts du Canada  ONTARIO ARTS COUNCIL / CONSEIL DES ARTS DE L'ONTARIO

 Canadian Heritage / Patrimoine canadien 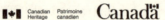 Canada

The publisher gratefully acknowledges the support of the Canada Council for the Arts and the Ontario Arts Council for its publishing program. We acknowledge the financial support of the Government of Canada through the Canada Book Fund (CBF) for our publishing activities, and the Government of Ontario through the Ontario Media Development Corporation, an agency of the Ontario Ministry of Culture, and the Ontario Book Publishing Tax Credit Program.

LIBRARY AND ARCHIVES CANADA CATALOGUING IN PUBLICATION

Hunter, Martin, 1933–
The critic : and other stories / Martin Hunter.

Issued also in electronic formats.
ISBN 978-1-77086-088-9

1. Title.

PS8565.U58C75 2013   C813'.54   C2013-900476-9

Cover art: Portrait of Herbert Whittaker by Barker Fairley, courtesy of the Arts & Letters Club.
Cover design: Angel Guerra/Archetype
Interior text design: Tannice Goddard, Soul Oasis Networking
Printer: Trigraphik LBF

Printed and bound in Canada.

The interior of this book is printed on 30% post-consumer waste recycled paper.

CORMORANT BOOKS INC.
390 Steelcase Road East, Markham, Ontario, L3R 1G2
www.cormorantbooks.com

CONTENTS

THE HARRISON SISTERS | 1

THE CRITIC | 23

LEFT BANK | 41

BREAKING OUT | 61

ANGEL CAKE | 71

THE MATING GAME | 85

LENORE | 109

WILL YOU JOIN THE DANCE? | 123

MONTREAL REVISITED | 139

THE BISHOP'S VISITOR | 149

WRITER'S BLOCK | 157

REUNION | 177

ACKNOWLEDGEMENTS | 201

THE HARRISON SISTERS

Agnes awoke to the sound of the pine trees swaying in the wind. She lay back and drank it in, as if she could taste it — like camomile tea. A silly thought from a silly old woman. She loved this sound; she had listened to it every summer as far back as she could remember. She made little sniffling sounds in imitation of the wind in the tall pines. Outside her window she heard the sound of a lawnmower and thought for a moment it was Sean, the local farm boy, who used to cut their grass, but Sean was long gone.

"*T'as bien dormi, ma p'tite?*" Emmeline hovered over her, a grumpy but concerned she-bear. Agnes responded with a rather curt "*Oui, merci.*" She didn't really speak French, but thought it polite to communicate with Emmeline in her own language. She always slept well and Emmeline knew it. Agnes thought Emmeline was an interfering old busybody, but she knew that if she was going to spend two months at the cottage every summer she had to have someone to look after her. Her older sister had insisted on it and no doubt she was right.

The Harrisons had owned a cottage in the Gatineau for three generations. It had been built by Agnes's grandfather as a fishing camp. Agnes's father, Harry, had summered there as a boy, spending at least a month every year until his recent death. Agnes loved the cottage, the lake, the surrounding countryside with its tumbledown barns, dirt roads, and covered bridges. She loved being there with her father and even Emmeline, who often picked raspberries and blueberries while Agnes sat on a campstool in front of her easel and painted.

Harry had often driven her to some spot that had caught her fancy: an old stone house or abandoned mill, a small waterfall tumbling over a ruined dam, a tiny hamlet with three houses and a general store. The local people came to know her and would view her work with the pleasure of familiarity, flattered that she had singled out their little corner of the world. Harry had employed some of the local people to do repairs or thin out the brush; he had been known to be a generous patron and the local people felt a pang of sympathy for his afflicted daughter.

Agnes's mother had died giving birth to a daughter with both cerebral palsy and a cleft palate. Agnes soon established herself as her father's favourite. Harry Harrison had two sturdy teenage sons, Colin and Bert, and an equally sturdy daughter, whom the family called Toots. The boys were protective of their youngest and disabled sister. Toots was secretly jealous, but suppressed her feelings. She took on the burden of running the town house, a sizeable Victorian mansion on Pine Avenue in Montreal.

In the summer, Toots had the house in town to herself. She enjoyed being on her own. She gave parties for her school friends and their brothers and was asked to their parties in return. She acquired a beau of her own, Daniel, who worked in an investment house. One September, when Harry and Agnes returned from the cottage, Toots invited Daniel to dinner. Harry peppered him with questions about politics and the state of the economy, music, and the theatre. Daniel found himself at a loss to respond to this grilling. He was not an intellectual and he knew it. He left soon after dinner, excusing himself by saying he had an early meeting the next morning. Toots rounded on her father, accusing him of trying to make Daniel uncomfortable. Harry responded that he was attempting to take the young man's measure. "I would hope you could do better, Toots." Toots went up to her bedroom, where she stared out the window at nothing in particular, chain-smoking. The next time she invited Daniel to dinner, he declined. They met two or three times after that before he told her he was moving to Toronto.

At age seventy Harry retired. Now he could spend the whole summer at the cottage with Agnes. He urged Toots to join them, but she opted to go to Murray Bay with friends. Colin had taken a job in South Africa. Bert came to visit with his fiancée, a pretty Scottish girl with red hair who took the trouble to cultivate Harry. He took her out in a canoe and taught her how to paddle, which she quickly mastered. She gave Emmeline a break by cooking dinner and putting a very appetizing meal on the table, including a raspberry pie. Harry indicated to Bert that she was a real find. "That girl's a keeper." The young people went back to the city, pleased to have his blessing.

Later that summer Harry had a stroke. He was taken to hospital in Ottawa, but after two weeks was released. His left arm was paralyzed and he would have to walk with a stick, but his brain had not been affected. Toots had come up to Ottawa to help care for him and take him back to Montreal. But Harry was adamant that he wanted to go back to the cottage for the rest of the summer. "Who's going to look after you?" Toots asked, as if that settled the matter. She discovered that Emmeline and Agnes had engaged a local boy, Sean Lefebvre, to come in every day for several hours.

Sean had been hired earlier in the summer to paint the shed and Harry had taken a liking to him. Toots tried to disrupt this arrangement, but Agnes stood up to her. "I know what Father wants better than you do," she said. Toots had to admit to herself that this was true. She was surprised that Agnes could be so strong-willed, but decided not to oppose her sister directly. Instead she determined to stay at the cottage to keep an eye on things.

It seemed to Agnes inevitable that Toots would not take to Sean, but he made a play for her. He admired her smart clothes and enjoyed her tart comments. She set out to brighten up the cottage with new curtains and slipcovers for the furniture. Sean went shopping with her in Ottawa, helping to choose fabrics and persuading her to buy a pop-up toaster and a blender. Toots enjoyed being seen in the company of this good-looking young man, even if he was half a head shorter and twenty years younger.

Sean established a strong rapport with Agnes when she discovered he had a real talent as a draftsman. His sketches of birds and farm animals were detailed and accurate. They also had a certain delicacy. Before long, the two went on sketching expeditions together in the afternoon.

Toots allowed Sean to drive her car. She told herself she was happy that Agnes had found companionship with this nice young man. When it came time to go back to Montreal, the sisters discussed the possibility of Sean coming to live with them in the city. Sean declined. He appreciated the offer and said he was tempted, but he was needed to work on the family farm and he wanted to finish high school.

That winter, Harry had another stroke; after two weeks in the Montreal General, he succumbed. The Church of St. Andrew and St. Paul was crowded at his funeral. Agnes wept as the mourners sang "O God, our help in ages past," but Toots looked straight ahead, bright-eyed and resolute, her chin trembling a little. Bert delivered the eulogy, praising his father's integrity and sense of fairness as a businessman. After the burial, family friends gathered at the Mount Stephen Club. Bert was duly commended for his oratory by the old man's friends as ice cubes rattled in their whisky glasses.

Two days later both Toots and Agnes received letters from Sean. They were simple expressions of his admiration for Mr. Harrison, who had been helpful to the Lefebvre family and whom he had come to think of as a second father. "He writes very nicely," said Toots. "He has a beautiful nature," said Agnes. Toots agreed, though she would never have said such a thing herself.

The will was read by Mr. Harrison's lawyer in the library of the Pine Avenue house. Their father's considerable fortune was divided equally among the four siblings. Toots inherited the Montreal house with the provision that she allow Agnes to live there as long as she wished, and Agnes was left the cottage. They all thought this was a fair division, typical of their father's good sense, though Toots secretly wondered about the advisability of Agnes controlling her own money — not that she had ever shown any signs of extravagance.

In June, Agnes prepared for her annual trip to the cottage. She asked Toots to spend the summer with her. Toots said she wanted to stay in Montreal. She had plans to redecorate the house, but would come to the cottage in a few weeks. Agnes could take Emmeline with her for the whole summer. But Emmeline didn't drive. Agnes had a bright idea. She would ask Sean to come to Montreal by bus and drive her and Emmeline to the cottage in their father's Packard. Sean would be available to work for them all summer. He could repaint the porch and drive them into the village to shop, or into Ottawa. Toots approved of this plan. She only wished she could have Sean with her in Montreal to help with the redecoration of the house. He had a good eye.

Sean agreed to stay with the family in Montreal for a week before they drove north. He shopped with Toots and afterwards explored the city on his own. Several nights he came home late. Toots heard him coming in and sneaking up the staircase in his stocking feet. She wondered if Agnes had heard him too, but decided it was better not to mention it. Sean was eighteen now and it was natural for him to be curious about the city's nightlife. It somehow made him seem more appealing. The idea found Toots surprised at her own romantic imagination. But of course she kept her thoughts and feelings about Sean to herself. He was just a kid, a half-Irish, half-French farm boy, whose English was coloured by traces of both parental influences.

When Toots arrived at the cottage two weeks later, she quickly realized Agnes was in a state of excitement. After dinner, as they sat on the screened porch looking out over the lake, Toots puffed on her cigarette and Agnes opened up to her sister. "I've made a decision. I'm going to Europe. What do you think of that?"

"I'm completely flabbergasted. What would you want to do that for?"

"To see the art in Paris and Florence and Rome."

"You can see pictures right here."

"It's not the same. I want to sit in little cafés and watch the people. Ride on a boat down the Seine …"

"But you don't speak French or Italian." Toots refrained

from pointing out that many people couldn't understand Agnes when she spoke English. Toots had gotten used to her distorted speech, but even their brother Bert sometimes had difficulty making out what Agnes was saying.

"Now that I have money of my own ..."

"I'm sure Father wouldn't have wanted you wasting it on something like this." She stubbed out her cigarette and immediately lit another.

"He'd be happy to know I was using it to do something I've always wanted."

"You can't go travelling by yourself. Surely you realize that."

"Sean is willing to come with me."

"How is he going to pay for that?"

"I'll pay. He'll make all the arrangements."

"Using your money."

"We pay him to work for us here. What's the difference?"

"All the difference in the world. What will people think? You travelling around with a boy fifteen years your junior. The church would be full of it."

There was a pause while Agnes let this sink in. She didn't care about the people at the church, but she could understand that this was important to Toots. Then she turned to Toots with a bright little smile. "You should come with us."

"Me? Why would I want to do that? I don't give a hang about art."

"You like pretty things. I'm sure the shopping must be wonderful."

"I couldn't shop in Paris. I don't speak French."

"But Sean does. You love shopping with him."

"I don't want to talk any more about this now." Toots stubbed out her cigarette and got up. "I'm going to bed."

Agnes sat in the growing dark, looking out on the lake, hoping to hear the call of a loon. She could hear Toots clomping around in her bedroom. Toots was something of a nighthawk. It wouldn't be easy for her to settle down in her bed at this hour. Agnes felt she had made her case well. She hummed to herself with satisfaction when Emmeline came to help her get ready for bed.

The next morning, Toots was up early and as soon as Sean put in an appearance she bore down on him. "What's this crazy nonsense I hear about you going to Europe with Agnes?"

"I think it will be good for her."

"What do you know about it? Agnes can't manage to look after herself."

"I'll look after her."

"You can put her to bed, get her up in the morning? Give her her bath?"

"Why not? I do for my young brothers and sisters."

"That's completely different. Surely you're not ignorant of …"

"What?"

"Decent human behaviour." She paused, waiting for an answer. Sean smiled at her.

"I suppose this was your idea. You put her up to it."

"She jumped to it the minute I mentioned it."

"I thought so. Did she talk about me coming with you?"

"You want to come? That will be good." His smile grew wider.

"You're bold as brass. You'll say anything."

"I say what I think you want hear."

"You admit it."

"You will love Paris very much. The bistros, the shops. *La plus élégante ville du monde.*"

"I'm not going to sit here and listen to a lot of hooey. You'd better get busy chopping kindling."

Sean's smile didn't waver as he turned to go. He started down the path and turned back, still smiling.

Toots was in a rare state of confusion. The idea of going to Paris had appeal, but was also frightening. She would be out of her element. Sean would be in control; that would be intolerable, especially now that he had revealed himself to be an opportunist. She lit another cigarette and headed for the kitchen. She wished she could confide in Emmeline, but that wasn't an option. She sat with a mug of coffee and smoked. Then she wrote a letter to her brother Bert.

Agnes was pleased as always to see Bert and even more pleased to see his daughter, Betty Jo. She showed her niece some of her paintings and asked her to pick one she would like to have for herself. Betty Jo chose a scene with sparrows perched on the branches of a forsythia tree in the garden of the house on Pine Avenue. Agnes didn't think this was her best work, but she was pleased the girl liked it.

"When are you going to paint me, Aunt Agnes?"

"Oh, I couldn't do that, dear. I don't paint people."

"Why not?"

"I'm not good enough. I've tried, but it never seems to come out right."

"Maybe you should take some lessons."

"Maybe I should."

"Run along now, Betty Jo," said Bert, as he settled into the rocking chair that had been his father's favourite.

"Why don't you look in the top drawer of the chiffonier in my bedroom, dear. There's a garnet necklace that belonged to your grandmother. I've been meaning to give it to you for some time, but I keep forgetting to bring it to Montreal."

Betty Jo disappeared into the cottage. Bert looked out across the lake for a moment. "I might as well come right to the point. Toots has told me about your idea of going to Europe with this young rascal Sean."

"He isn't a rascal."

"Toots says he's untrustworthy. He more or less admitted to her he thought up this scheme. I'm afraid he's only after your money."

"I don't believe that. He's a good boy. He's an artist."

"A con artist from the sound of it. I'm sure when you think about this, you'll see how unsuitable the whole thing is."

"Why unsuitable?"

"Travelling with a man many years younger than you."

"But if Toots comes with us …"

"Toots doesn't want to go to Paris. She's terrified you'll come down with something and she won't know what to do to help you. You've both led very sheltered lives and we all know how delicate your health is. We try not to mention it, but we're all worried ..."

Agnes looked at him with an expression he'd never seen before. Could it be defiance?

"Please, Agnes, take my word for it. Toots and I both want what's best for you. We always have. You know that. And I have an alternative. Why don't you and Toots take Betty Jo to New York for a week? There are lots of museums there, and shops, and good restaurants, and ..."

Betty Jo came back. She had found the necklace and also a long braid of human hair. "Look at this," she said, holding it up for Agnes to admire. "Is it yours?"

"Yes. I used to have hair that hung down to my waist. I cut it off years ago. I'd forgotten all about it. I don't know why I didn't throw it out."

"Can I have it?"

"If you want it, dear. What will you do with it?"

"It's almost exactly the same colour as my hair. I could wear it."

"On Hallowe'en?" asked her father.

"Oh, Daddy. No, to the school formal."

"We've just been planning a trip. Aunt Toots and Aunt Agnes are going to take you for a holiday to New York. Would you like that?"

"That sounds fabulous."

"All settled then. It's your graduation present, so you'd better get good marks." He got up from his chair. "I'll tell Toots. It'll be a load off her mind. And then you and I are going for a swim, young lady, so you'd better get into your swimsuit."

AGNES WAS LEFT ALONE on the porch. She realized she'd been out-manoeuvred. She was not used to being disappointed because she never expected much. Even with her painting, she had long ago decided to concentrate on what she knew she could do. She wished Sean had never thought up this idea of going to Europe. Now she would have to tell him it was off. The idea of his disappointment was more painful than anything she felt for herself.

Bert and Betty Jo stayed for two days and then went back to Montreal. Over the years, they had been infrequent visitors at the cottage; Bert's wife had inherited a farm in the Eastern Townships where they spent most of their summers. The subject of the European trip was not mentioned again until after they left, when Toots asked Agnes if she would like her to inform Sean of the change in plans. Agnes said she would rather deal with it herself. Toots would have liked to be in on the meeting, but decided it might be good for Agnes to handle it on her own. She could always step in and lay down the law if Agnes faltered. She toyed with the idea of listening from the next room but decided this was unworthy of a family that prided itself on mutual trust. When she saw Sean cycling along the path the next day she decided to go into town to shop for groceries.

Sean said good morning to Agnes, who watched him intently as he got his gardening tools out of the shed. Something must have hinted to him that Agnes was unusually tense because he stopped and smiled at her.

"I was thinking we could plant some more rosebushes in that circular bed," she said.

Sean shrugged. "You will not be here to see them."

"We're not going."

Sean looked at her, puzzled. "What do you mean?"

"I'm not going to Europe with you. I'm not strong enough. It isn't practical. And it isn't suitable."

"Who said this to you?"

"My brother and Toots."

"Toots is jealous." Sean stood for a moment, slapping the palm of his left hand with a trowel.

"I've disappointed you. I'm sorry."

"Yes, you disappoint me. I thought you had more ... *esprit*."

"I want you to go, Sean. I will pay for it."

"I cannot do that."

"Please. It will make me happy to know someone is making good use of my money. I have much more than I need. You must work hard at your drawing and learn all you can. Promise me." She took an envelope out of her bag and handed it to him.

Sean stared at the envelope for a moment, then put it in the pocket of his overalls. He took both her hands in his and kissed her on the cheek. Agnes felt a little shiver run through her. The Harrisons were not a family given to kissing.

"I will write you many letters," he said. He climbed on his bicycle and rode off down the path.

When Toots returned from grocery shopping, Agnes was still sitting on the porch looking out over the lake. Toots set her shopping bags on the table.

"Well?"

"I told him."

"I suppose you blamed me."

"No. I decided you were right."

"How did he take it?"

"He's disappointed. Naturally."

"He'll get over it." Toots gave her sister a reassuring pat on the shoulder and carried her bags out to the kitchen. Agnes was surprised to realize she felt relief as much as anything.

Ten days later, Toots was packing up to go back to the city. She paused on the porch to have a cigarette when she saw Sean coming up the path on his bike. He was wearing a brown corduroy jacket and a brightly coloured tie of blue and yellow.

"You're all done up like a dog's dinner," Toots said. And then, seeing his puzzled expression, she added, "You look very handsome."

"Thank you. I am coming to say goodbye."

"You're going away somewhere?"

"Europe. You know I want to go."

"Sit down. I'll get Agnes."

Sean looked at the half-finished painting on Agnes's easel and recognized the old church at St. Polycarpe-de-Belmont. She had depicted the town square during morning mass in the winter with sleighs and horses waiting for the worshippers and two or three men smoking their pipes, waiting for the elevation of the Host to go inside.

Agnes came out of the house in her dressing gown of pink satin embroidered with Chinese flowers. Sean walked up to her and gave her a big hug.

"You're going to have a wonderful adventure. Remember, you promised to write to me."

"For sure."

"I'm driving to Montreal. I could give you a lift," said Toots.

"Thank you. I have my bus ticket here. And I must take back my bike. I'm giving it to Stephane, my brother."

The three of them stood for a minute not knowing what to say.

"I like your picture. It is of your best." He smiled at Agnes. "I must go. Papa will drive me to the bus." He took Toots's hand and kissed it. She smiled at him, half delighted, half embarrassed. He went down the steps and picked up his bike, turned to wave, and was gone.

Toots lit a cigarette and exhaled. "How can he afford to go to Europe?" When Agnes didn't reply, she said, "You gave him the money. How much?"

"Five thousand dollars."

"Are you crazy? I knew it was a mistake for Daddy to let you have control of your money."

"Daddy would be pleased. He liked Sean."

"He should have left him something in his will."

"He would have if he'd thought if it."

"You're a fool, Agnes." Toots's face flushed. "I shouldn't have said that. I'm sorry."

"It's all right. I'd rather be a fool than mean."

Toots didn't know what Agnes meant by this. She stubbed out her cigarette and walked into the house to finish her packing. Agnes looked at her picture with a little smile of satisfaction.

AGNES CONTINUED TO PAINT both at the cottage and in Montreal. A friend introduced her to a gallery owner on Bishop Street who took three of her paintings on consignment. They sold quite quickly and Agnes signed a contract to supply the gallery with a certain number of paintings each year. "Not too many; that way we can gradually drive the price up." Agnes didn't care about the price but she was happy to take her dealer's advice.

Sean wrote regularly, once a week at first. He described Paris, its buildings and gardens and galleries. He said little of his social life but it seemed that he had made friends. After some months he settled in London, where he had been taken on as a protégé by an older painter, Oliver Messel. Agnes had never heard of him, but she gathered that he was able to arrange for Sean to get work that would pay him something. She wrote back and, although she had nothing much to say, she ornamented her letters with little sketches of birds and squirrels and rabbits. Gradually Sean's letters became less frequent and she understood he was becoming absorbed into a life of his own. She was happy for him.

Toots always asked to see Sean's letters. She enjoyed reading them, but when Agnes suggested she should write to Sean, she replied that she had nothing to say to him. Emmeline retired, but still came to the cottage in the summer. Toots hired a younger, more energetic woman who could drive. Toots felt that she could leave Agnes to go on short trips of a week or two, sometimes with Betty Jo, sometimes with a friend her own age. Mostly she went to New York and returned with new clothes and shoes. She confessed to Agnes that she had over forty pairs of shoes, some of which she had worn only two or three times.

At the age of forty-six Toots was diagnosed with lung cancer. "I suppose it was all that smoking," she said with a bitter little laugh. "Well, I had to have some pleasure in life, didn't I?" When she was offered a radical cure of radiation and told that her hair would all fall out, she refused treatment. Her funeral in the Church of St. Andrew and St. Paul was attended by old friends of the family, but not many others. Her clothes were given to the church and Bert and his wife helped clear out the house on Pine Avenue and sell it. They installed Agnes in a spacious apartment on Côte-des-Neiges. Bert visited Agnes once a week for tea. "It's too bad Toots never took up charity work," said Bert. "She could have done a lot of good."

"She was very good to Betty Jo."

"Speaking of whom — Betty Jo is engaged. Nice young man. A lawyer with a good firm. We're very pleased."

"I'm glad," said Agnes. "You must tell her to come and choose a painting for a wedding present. And perhaps they'd like to spend their honeymoon at the cottage."

"That's very kind of you, Agnes, but I believe they're going to the Caribbean. It's all the rage now."

"Give her my love." Agnes was happy for Betty Jo.

AGNES WAS TAKING A little break, dozing on the porch swing, when she heard the sound of a car drive up and park behind the cottage. "Anybody home?" called out a voice, followed by a middle-aged man walking along the path. He was smartly dressed in white duck trousers with a tennis sweater draped over his shoulders. He had rather longish hair and a salt-and-pepper beard. "Everything looks just the same."

Agnes started at him.

"You don't remember me? Sean Lefebvre."

"You've changed quite a lot."

"You haven't changed a bit."

"You were always a smooth talker, Sean. Come and sit down. Miss Matthers will bring us tea." She picked up a little bell and rang it.

"You're still painting?"

"Yes. Are you?"

"Not your kind. I'm a decorative painter. I do faux marble. Faux wood grains. Everything faux. And a lot of tromping. I'm very well paid. And I've got to work in some of the grandest stately homes in England." He chuckled a bit self-deprecatingly. "But I'm not famous like you."

"Famous?"

"You've got paintings hanging in the Musée des Beaux-Arts, the National Gallery …"

Miss Matthers arrived with tea and sugar tarts and set them on the table.

"This is Sean Lefebvre. He grew up on a farm right near here. And now he's a painter in England."

"Well, I never," chirped Miss Matthers. "Pleased to meet you."

"It all began with Agnes. She gave me my start."

Miss Matthers smiled and scuttled back to her kitchen.

"Have you been to see your family?"

"They moved to Temiskaming. I'm on my way to see them now."

"You've lost your accent."

"I worked at it. When I was first in London, people thought my accent was cute, but I wanted to be accepted."

"And you have been?"

"I have to say yes." There was something a little bit aggressive about Sean that bothered Agnes slightly. As though he felt he had to justify himself — maybe to justify her five thousand dollars. Well, it had been money well spent, she thought as she looked across at him. But she didn't quite know how to tell him this.

"It's a pity Toots isn't here to see you. She died of cancer."

"She came to see me in London."

"She did?"

"She didn't tell you? She came twice. The second time I took her to Italy. It was quite … romantic in a way, but …"

"I'm glad for Toots's sake. She didn't have a lot of fun in her life."

"I'm afraid you're right. I was happy to do something for her, but ... the gap was too wide." He paused. "She saw that."

"She was always practical."

They sat together drinking tea and then Agnes showed him some of her recent paintings.

"You just get better and better."

"I do the same things over and over. But I'm too old to try new things. I've learned what I can do."

"I know what you mean. I tried to be a serious painter, but I guess I just don't have it. Sometimes I've thought if I came back here I might somehow reconnect but ... it's just not in the cards. Would you like to go for a spin in my rented convertible?"

"No, dear. It's enough just to have seen you."

"I'll tell you what. I'll come by on my way back to Montreal if you'll promise to let me drive you around for a bit. Deal?"

She smiled at him. "I'll be happy to see you again if you have time."

Sean stood, gave her a hug, walked back to the car, and drove off. Agnes sat on the swing and thought of Toots in Italy. She felt happy for Toots, happy that she'd had the strength of character to grab a few moments of pleasure. Just as she was happy that Sean had been able to take her gift and use it to make something of himself. And suddenly she had an idea. She could leave the cottage to Sean. It might inspire him to paint again. She felt certain Toots would approve.

THE CRITIC

Charles Minton claimed he had heard bombs exploding over London during the Great War. If so, he had a remarkable memory, for he was only four-and-a-half years old when it ended in Allied victory. Thirty years later he was living with his widowed mother in Montreal's Notre-Dame-de-Grâce district. He had won a bursary to the École des Beaux-Arts, where he studied graphic design. A fellow student, a very stylish and "fast" young woman with whom he was infatuated for a time, introduced him to an amateur theatre group; he began designing and painting their sets, though his mother soon sent his sometime-girlfriend packing. He managed to get a bit of freelance work drawing for the *Montreal Star*, at a time when newspapers featured printed sketches of criminals. He occasionally contributed theatre reviews as a stringer. In 1939 he was rejected by the army because of his flat feet and poor eyesight, but he contributed to the war effort by drawing patriotic cartoons for the paper.

When Charles was offered the job of film critic by the *Toronto Telegram* shortly after the end of the war, he accepted with alacrity. Not only was the salary considerably more than he had been earning in Montreal, but he knew it was time to get away from his overbearing mother. She had been a strong supporter of his artistic interests and ambitions, but her constant advice and sharp comments now irritated rather than encouraged him. He also needed to put some distance between himself and his closest friend, Simon, for whom he had entertained an unrequited passion for half a decade. Simon was married with two small sons. He was aware that Charles was attracted to him and made it clear that they could not be lovers. He respected Charles's considerable gifts as a stage designer and encouraged him to believe that he would have greater opportunities to exercise his talents in Toronto. But, as Charles's recent forays into directing were beginning to challenge his own established mastery in that field, Simon's advice was not entirely altruistic.

IT HAPPENED THAT CHARLES'S Toronto editor, who lived in a large house in the Annex, was looking for someone to rent his third floor, which contained a small and attractive apartment. It was partly furnished with slightly battered second-hand furniture and had a pleasant view onto a street lined with huge elm and chestnut trees. Charles agreed to take it, and decided to pick up a few additional pieces of second-hand furniture at Ward-Price's; he decorated his new home by hanging his own costume sketches and two posters from Picasso's blue period.

At the auction house he found himself sitting beside a woman in her late forties. She was conservatively dressed and had an air of distinction. Seeing Charles marking up his program, she commented on several of the articles in a knowledgeable way and encouraged him to buy a round French-Canadian pedestal table, which she said was early nineteenth century and an original design. When she confided to him that she worked as a curator at the Royal Ontario Museum, he was inclined to take her advice. She was interested to learn that Charles was a journalist, new to the city. She invited him for drinks the following Thursday.

At her house, which was just a few blocks away from his flat, he met a small group of her friends: a professor of history, a curator at the Art Gallery of Toronto, and a poetess who also taught at the university. They were just the sort of people Charles had hoped to meet, cultivated and obviously of some social standing. His hostess, whose name was Fredericka, was known to her friends as Freddy. Her house had a certain shabby elegance; it had belonged to her family for two generations and was full of interesting and unusual things: Japanese prints brought home by an uncle who had been a missionary; silver and cut glass inherited from her Anglo-Irish grandmother; paintings by her sister who was on friendly terms with two members of the Group of Seven; Turkish kilims and Egyptian brass collected by her husband, who had been a diplomat specializing in the Middle East.

The conversation centred on travel in Europe, which people had begun to visit again; there was much comparison with what they remembered from the thirties, most of it disparaging of present conditions. Freddy herself had just returned from Egypt, her husband's last post before his recent death. Charles, having recently visited London with his mother, was able to contribute to the conversation.

After about half an hour they were joined by Freddy's nineteen-year-old son, William. He was a tall, broad-shouldered lad with jet-black hair and amber-coloured eyes, and had just started university. He had brought along his girlfriend Delia, a tiny young woman with red hair and an ample bosom, who although initially seeming shy soon let it be known she had ambitions as an actress. Something about William reminded Charles of Simon — perhaps the candour of his gaze, at once innocent and challenging.

When Delia discovered that Charles had experience as a stage designer she suggested that he might like to design the forthcoming college production she was helping to produce. Her college drama club had obtained the amateur rights for *Summer and Smoke*, which Charles had recently seen on Broadway with Geraldine Page in the lead role. This clinched it for Delia. She undertook to arrange for Charles to meet the college theatre committee the following week. Charles asked William if he was interested in acting and received only a shy smile and a shrug.

Charles would soon come to realize that, although William was the better looking of the pair, Delia was the dominant partner in their relationship. She arranged to have coffee with Charles at a student hangout on Bloor Street and grilled him about his theatrical experience. Charles, by now ensconced as a journalist, was used to asking the questions; but, realizing that Delia was a forceful young woman and that he had made a strong impression on her, he held back and submitted to her interrogation. He liked strong women and understood that they enjoyed doing things for him. At the same time they seemed to know intuitively that although he was happy to accept their offers of assistance (indeed he played up his lack of practicality to gain their sympathy) he would not make emotional demands of them. In the course of his interview with Delia he cannily revealed that he had recently started to direct plays in Montreal and had achieved some success, especially with his female actors.

Delia had been planning to direct the Tennessee Williams play herself but instead put Charles forward as both director and designer, assuring the committee they would be lucky to get him. And so it was decided with a minimum of wrangling. Sometimes the pieces fall in place so easily, thought Charles.

Charles might have realized that Delia would audition for Alma, the shy, reclusive spinster from a Southern rectory who is the central character of Williams's play and whose only emotional outlet is singing in the church choir. She didn't meet his idea of the character, whom he thought should be frail and flighty rather than determined. When he confided this to Freddy she pointed out that Delia had sung in Healey Willan's choir for years and had a very nice voice. She was also rather socially awkward and consequently insecure under her aggressive exterior. Charles took her comments to heart, even though he was loath to admit that Freddy might be more perceptive than he. He auditioned Delia and realized that Freddy's assessment of the girl was shrewdly accurate. He decided to go with her. He explained that he was casting her "against type" and that she would have to work hard to catch the essence of Alma's character. He had already decided to cast William as John, the handsome doctor whom Alma has a crush on. Here again he would be reversing the real-life situation, for he could see plainly that it was William who was pursuing Delia. He took a perverse enjoyment in going against conventional appearances.

The college students enjoyed Charles's rehearsals, which were relaxed and easygoing in the early stages. He insisted they call him by his first name, not Mr. Minton. He appeared not as a martinet, but rather a counsellor, who suggested they explore their own experience to come to an understanding of the characters they were playing. Often he would arrive ten or fifteen minutes late, saying he'd had to finish a column or an interview. He improvised a good deal, and seemed to have no preconceived plan. Although they were supposed to finish up at ten o'clock, the rehearsals usually ran on until eleven. Many of the actors would then repair to Diana Sweets, a restaurant on Bloor Street that stayed open until midnight. There they would drink black coffee and smoke cigarettes in imitation of the lifestyle they imagined prevailed among Parisian existentialists. They talked of the theatre of Anouilh and Cocteau and Giraudoux, which Charles had experienced firsthand. He had actually seen Sartre and Simone de Beauvoir drinking at the Café de Flore.

Sometimes Charles would invite Delia and William and one or two of his other favourite actors to his apartment for a nightcap. He would regale them with stories of actors he had seen or met in New York and London — Gertrude Lawrence, John Gielgud, Katharine Cornell, Charles Laughton, Noël Coward, the Lunts — until he ran out of whisky. Charles was a night-owl who went to bed late and rarely arose before noon. The students took this as a sign of a sophisticated, bohemian lifestyle; some of them imitated it, skipping breakfast in the college dining hall and getting up so late they also missed lunch.

As rehearsals progressed, the students began to see another side of Charles. They could not always understand his directions. He expected them to be quick on the uptake and did not care to explain his ideas. He became testy when they were slow learning their lines or forgot their blocking. He occasionally changed his conception of a scene entirely and if they did not immediately grasp the brilliance of his new idea he could grow sulky and stamp out of rehearsal. Delia would have to go outside where he was puffing on a cigarette and woo him back. He was particularly demanding with the technical people who were trying to realize his set and costume designs, which were often no more than brief sketches he had done on a paper napkin at Diana Sweets.

On the last week of rehearsal, Freddy came to a run-through. Afterwards she took Charles back to her house for a drink. She praised his work, but was not without criticism. She felt he had been wonderfully successful in shaping Delia's performance as she progressed from embarrassed girl to disappointed adult. But she was considerably less impressed by William's performance. She acknowledged that he was handsome and charming, but he lacked the essential recklessness of the character. "Of course, he's not really an actor." Charles was miffed; he had been quite captivated by William's performance. He had chosen him and he took her comments personally. He also wondered if the idea of her son becoming an actor worried Freddy. He understood it was not considered a suitable profession for a young man of his background.

During the next week Charles attacked William in rehearsal. "Can't you give me something wilder, less controlled?" he asked. "We'll do the scene again and try to be less sympathetic, more brutal." They repeated the scene, but brutal was not in William's repertoire. He could shout and stamp his feet, but he came across as a peevish child, not an impulsive rebel. "How was that?" he asked rather plaintively when they had finished the scene. "Let's take a break," said Charles and went outside for a cigarette.

Delia went out to join him. "He's doing the best he can."

"I know. That's the problem. Maybe you should reverse

roles, just for the hell of it. I'll bet you could show him a thing or two."

Delia shrugged. "I'm game."

"Why don't you suggest it?"

They went back and Delia explained the idea to William as if it were her own invention. He agreed to give it a try, but he was so embarrassed that he couldn't take in what Delia was doing. In an excess of zeal Delia slapped him. He looked at her in shock. "I'd never do that to a woman," he said. Charles realized this experiment was going nowhere and ended the rehearsal.

"I'm sorry, Charles," William said. "I guess I just don't understand what you want."

"Never mind. Go back to the way you were doing it," Charles said with a slight pout. He didn't go to Diana Sweets that night and a cloud hung over those who did.

IN ORDER TO ATTRACT an audience, Charles arranged for his newspaper to send someone to review the show, even though amateur and student productions were not often covered in the big dailies. The paper sent Edna Narroway, the books editor. She thought the play silly and trivial and denounced Tennessee Williams as a charlatan who would soon be forgotten. She praised Delia for giving some plausibility to an impossible role and dismissed William as wooden. The other main newspaper also sent a critic who gave Charles credit for trying to instill some life into a minor work by a minor playwright, whose popularity in the United States only showed how facile was the American understanding of the art of drama. He condemned the implausible Southern accents of the student actors, but commended Delia for her singing voice and her courage in tackling a difficult and thankless role.

The student audiences enjoyed the show and rewarded the players with laughs in unexpected places. Charles had not encouraged his actors to see the play as a comedy but now that they were getting laughs they began to play up this aspect of the script in subsequent performances, until by Saturday night they might as well having been performing *The Man Who Came to Dinner*.

There was a cast party at Freddy's, with a lavish spread including boeuf bourguignon, lasagna, and two salads. Freddy provided red and white wine and beer, but wisely did not offer her guests spirits. Even so, the theology student who was playing Alma's father passed out on the sofa and had to be taken back to the college and put to bed by two of the stagehands. Charles was presented with a gift, an umbrella, which he pretended to be delighted with. He was feeling peevish however and confided to Freddy that the production had not really come up to the standards of his work in Montreal. "You've given these kids a wonderful experience, Charles. You ought to be proud of yourself." He gave her a morose little smile and excused himself, saying he had a headache. He was disappointed in Freddy. Surely she could understand that he had artistic aspirations beyond providing a bit of fun to a bunch of amateur actors.

He walked home and consumed a third of a bottle of Scotch before going to bed.

Three days later, Charles was lying in bed in the morning with a newspaper when he heard a knock on the door. "Who is it?"

"William. Can I come in?"

"Of course. I'm afraid I'm still in bed."

William came in and perched on a hard wooden chair. He looked across at Charles with a serious expression.

"You can sit on the edge of the bed, if you like. It'll be more comfortable."

"I'm okay here."

"I could make you some coffee."

"I can't stay. I've got a class in twenty minutes."

"What's on your mind?"

"It's about Delia. I don't know if she's told you. Some guy who runs a theatre in Bermuda came to see the show. He's offered her a job there. She wants to take it."

"That's terrific."

"You think so? I mean, shouldn't she get her degree first? At least finish her year? She's only eighteen, you know. It's great that she had a success in one part, but she doesn't have any training. Suppose she goes down there and it turns out this was a fluke."

"She has talent."

"I suppose you're a better judge of that than I am."

"Yes, I am."

"I expected her mother would be dead set against it, but

she seems to think it's all delightful. She wants to go with her."

"She'll have a chaperone."

"Her mother's pretty flighty."

"It sounds as though you're the one who's dead set against it."

"I'm only trying to think in terms of her best interests."

"If she doesn't go, she will always regret it. If she really wants to be an actress, she shouldn't pass this up. These opportunities don't come along every day."

"Girls like Delia don't come along every day."

Charles got out of bed and walked over to William. "If you truly want what's best for Delia, let her go. If she really cares about you, she'll come back. If she doesn't, better to find out now. You'll find other girls. You're a very good-looking boy." He put his hand on William's shoulder.

William looked up at him. He got up and crossed to the door. "I have to go. Thanks for taking the time." He left.

Charles sighed and got back into bed.

Freddy asked Charles for dinner the following Sunday. "I know the theatres will be dark, so I can have you all to myself for the whole evening." She had prepared a Spanish fish dish, zarzuela, which she said translated as "an opera of seafood." With it, she served a bottle of Chablis, a better wine than Charles would normally have bought for himself. In fact he had brought with him a bottle of cheap Italian wine and was rather embarrassed to present it. When he apologized, saying he had not had time to go out to the liquor store to get something decent, Freddy said, "Never mind. I'll use it for cooking."

Over the dessert that followed, a light, creamy *île flottante*, she said, "I want to thank you for talking some sense into William. I know he'll get over Delia. And she would have been most unsuitable as a diplomat's wife. William is planning to follow in his father's footsteps. He'll need a nice, accommodating girl. Delia is headstrong and capricious, like her mother. I've known Mimsy since we were girls; she's always been irresponsible. Delia was a love child, fathered by some American tycoon who'd made a fortune from chewing gum. She met him on holiday in Cuba. Of course he went back to his wife after a year or two."

"Actually, I was thinking about what's best for Delia."

"Delia will be fine in Bermuda. It's quite a good company and I believe Trevor is quite smitten with her."

"Trevor?"

"The company's artistic director."

"You've been in Bermuda?"

"I have a sister there. Please don't misunderstand me. I wish Delia no ill. But I do not want William to be seriously involved with her." She looked at Charles levelly as she crumpled her napkin. "Have you heard from Mavor?"

"We're supposed to be having lunch next week."

"Good. I told him to go and see your show. He and his mother are starting a new theatre company. Semi-professional. He's got some good people lined up. I think he's going to offer you a show to direct."

"That's very good of you, Freddy."

"That's what friends are for. And I sense we're going to be great friends, you and I." She smiled across the table at him, as she finished off her wine. "I enjoy your company. I enjoy having a man to escort me to the theatre. And you —"

"Will be happy to escort you anywhere."

"So we understand each other. A little brandy before you go?"

And so it turned out. Freddy would entertain her friends and Charles would pour drinks. She was a skilled hostess who brought together interesting and often unusual combinations of guests, and she was also an adventurous cook. As Charles's circle of friends was limited and his only culinary accomplishment was instant coffee, he was duly appreciative.

When Freddy was invited to dinner parties or cocktail parties, Charles was her escort. Charles didn't drive, but Freddy was happy to chauffeur him in her slightly dilapidated Packard. As a third-generation Torontonian, whose grandfather had made a small fortune as a printer and publisher, she knew the people in Toronto who mattered and, before very long, Charles got to know them too. A few of them thought Charles was an upstart, but mostly they were glad Freddy had found an agreeable companion who could contribute to an intelligent conversation and had the manners of a gentleman. They asked his advice on what shows to see in London and New York. Occasionally they bought his costume sketches, which provided him with extra income to supplement his meagre directing fees and modest salary at the paper. Though they never discussed the matter again, both Freddy and Charles found the arrangement most satisfactory.

EIGHTEEN MONTHS LATER CHARLES went drinking with some friends at the Blue Cellar, a seedy actors' hangout on Bloor Street west of Spadina. On the wall was the same Picasso print of a naked boy leading a horse that Charles had hung up in his apartment. "It's a bit of a cliché," one of Charles's companions said and Charles made a mental note to replace it, perhaps with a print by Matisse.

Just before closing time, William appeared. He was wearing a dinner jacket, and the end of his bow tie had come undone and hung down from his open collar. He had obviously been drinking. When Charles offered to buy him a Scotch, he readily accepted. He had been at a dance and just taken his date home. He told Charles he was house-sitting for a friend of his mother's and asked him to come home for a nightcap. Charles was uncertain, but agreed. They walked together several blocks to a tiny townhouse on St. Nicholas Street. William opened the door, sat on the edge of the sofa, and took off his patent leather shoes. "They were Dad's and they're too damn tight."

"Even so, you look very dapper."

William poured them both a generous shot of whisky and downed his in two short gulps. Charles eyed him quizzically. "Have you heard from Delia recently?"

"Yeah. I was going to go to Bermuda and visit her. But it

turns out she married this guy Trevor. He must be ten years older than she is."

"She wrote me a month or so ago. She seems happy. She's getting good parts and she gets on with the other actors. They all love her mother."

"Yeah, well …" There was a pause as William lay back on the sofa and closed his eyes. Charles wondered whether he had passed out. He came over to the edge of the sofa and William opened his eyes. "You remember I came to see you one morning just before Delia took off. I sort of thought then that you wanted to …" There was a pause as they looked at each other. "I have this problem, see. I'm a pretty good student, except in philosophy. My professor told me he'd give me a good grade if I slept with him." There was another pause. "I've never had sex with a guy. I thought you might give me some pointers."

Charles turned away. When he looked back, William was standing in his white briefs. Charles was aware of the patch of dark hair on his chest and the thin line of hair leading down his stomach to the band of his briefs.

William came over to Charles. They kissed. William opened his mouth and pressed his tongue into Charles's mouth, but Charles pulled back. "That was nice, but that's as far as we're going. You'll figure out what to do next. If this story about your professor is really true. Now I'm getting out of here."

Charles turned back. "Good night, William," he said and shut the door behind him.

Walking back to his apartment, Charles congratulated

himself. He had not lost control. He had not endangered his relationship with Freddy, which was worth more to him than a few minutes of sexual pleasure with William, pretty as the lad was. And the lad was handsome, a feast for the eyes. No doubt that's why he had chosen to be a critic and a director rather than a player. He was satisfied with his choice.

LEFT BANK

"Do you think Rick is queer and doesn't know it?"
"No. He was captain of the soccer team."
"He acted in a few plays."
"He's a narcissist, but that's not the same thing." Sofia's tone was cool and deliberate. Brenda recognized her friend was not inclined to discuss the matter any further, although she would have liked to pursue it. She suspected Sofia and Rick were more than friends. She and Sofia were sitting in a café on the Left Bank drinking *café filtre*. They had been in Paris for two months, studying at the Sorbonne following graduation from Trinity College, where they had both studied French literature. Sofia had been the better student. Her mother was Italian; her fluency in that language was only to be expected. But her French accent was also excellent, partly the result of having spent two years in a convent school in Quebec.

Brenda was in awe of Sofia. Her father was wealthy, the president of a company that distilled a whisky sold around the world. His family had founded the company; he was the third generation. As a young man he had travelled in Europe and returned home with an Italian bride. Brenda had met Sofia's mother when she had been invited over for dinner and was impressed by her elegance and beauty. She would never have guessed that Mrs. Cheltenham was in fact a gypsy the young Mr. Cheltenham had met at a street festival in Naples. He had persuaded her to come back to his hotel and a week later they married. He had had to teach her how to use a fork when she ate dinner; up to that time she had only used a knife, which she'd kept in her garter.

Sofia was not a beauty like her mother. She was handsome in a slightly unusual way, with a prominent nose and heavy eyebrows. But at Trinity she had never been without a boyfriend. Her father had given a coming-out ball for her at the York Club, which was attended by the sons of important businessmen, lawyers, and doctors. Almost every Saturday night she went to parties at the more prestigious fraternities on St. George Street and had spent several holidays with friends of her family in Bermuda and Barbados. Brenda knew she was not in the same league as Sofia. The year she came out, her mother had thrown a cocktail party in their ramshackle house in the Annex. Only half of that year's debutantes showed up and about a third of the young men.

"You're meeting Rick for dinner, aren't you?"

"We're expecting you to join us."

"I don't want to be a spare wheel."

"Don't be silly. It's not as if I have anything going with Rick. He's just an old friend of my brother's."

"What's he doing in Paris?"

"Improving his French. Hoping to be taken on as junior reporter with the *Herald-Tribune*."

"How likely is that?"

"He was on the masthead of the *Varsity* and he writes well. But I can't imagine how he passed his exams. He spent all his time partying."

"You did a fair bit yourself."

"Yes, but I read the texts we were assigned."

Sofia had graduated with firsts. Brenda was content with high seconds. She had gone out with a young man from a good family, a Zet, and had expected that he might propose to her. When the appropriate moment arrived, and her expectations were high, he explained that he had signed up with the navy for a three-year stint.

Sofia suggested she and Brenda go to Paris for graduate work. Brenda approached her father, who was skeptical of the value of further study for his daughter. But impressed by the eminence of Sofia's father, he agreed to come up with the money to pay Brenda's fees and lodging in Paris.

The two girls roomed together with a widow on a tiny street in the seventh arrondissement. They had a small sitting room and a kitchen with a bathtub in it — they didn't have to use the communal bathroom down the hall. Brenda was surprised that Sofia didn't object to this rather primitive accommodation. She had brought with her a very limited wardrobe, tweed skirts and sweaters — none of the ball gowns she had worn to parties in Toronto. Aware of the gap in their family incomes, Sofia treated Brenda as an equal. They had been boarders together at Ovenden in the forties. In their final year, the headmistress had allowed Sofia to go to dances, even in the middle of the week. Brenda would never have dared to request the same privileges.

Their landlady in the seventh arrondissement, Mme. Dudevant, was a woman in her fifties. She claimed to be a descendant of George Sand. She liked both girls, but took a particular interest in Sofia. Over the course of conversations the two women conducted three afternoons a week, Sofia learned about Mme. Dudevant's past. The older woman had confided to her that she had been married to a slightly younger man who worked for a bank. In the thirties he had been posted to Saigon and after a few months she had joined him there. She had settled into Vietnam happily, learned some of the language, and made friends with a number of Vietnamese. Her husband had insisted she return to France when the Japanese invaded China. He had joined the Free French under de Gaulle and been parachuted into France to do undercover work for the Resistance. He was shot by the Nazis.

After his death, Mme. Dudevant gave music lessons and rented rooms to students. She was a woman of cultivation, and played the cello. She rarely went out and seemed to have few friends. Sofia invited her to several concerts; she had studied piano and was quite discerning about contemporary classical French music. Mme. Dudevant had been fluent in English as a girl, but her command of the language had become rusty through disuse. She was particularly interested in learning current expressions. They discussed art and politics but also to some extent their personal lives. Sofia confided that she had a boyfriend, a young Italian student whom she had met while browsing at Shakespeare and Co.

"You love him?"

"He's very handsome and amusing. But I'm engaged to a young man back in Canada."

"He is not so amusing?"

"He's charming and very rich."

Mme. Dudevant smiled, but made no comment.

The girls' dinner with Rick took place at the Brasserie Lipp. Rick was showing off. "Let's start with champers." Like many Trinity boys, he had picked up certain British affectations.

Sofia teased him. "Are we supposed to be impressed?"

"I should jolly well hope so. You know Sartre and de Beauvoir often dine here."

"You think you'd recognize them? And, if you did, would you have the nerve to go up and speak to them?"

"Of course. I'm going to be a journalist, I have to be aggressive about getting interviews."

Sofia then pointed to a middle-aged woman eating alone. It was the Canadian writer Mavis Gallant. She encouraged Rick to ask her for an interview. He declined; he had never heard of her and had never read her work.

"That's a cop-out."

"Why don't you go and talk to her?"

"Maybe I will." Sofia stood up and walked over to Mme. Gallant's table, where it was evident she was asked to sit down.

She was gone for fifteen minutes. When she came back she said, "Guess who else I saw?"

"Albert Camus?"

"Professor Grimshaw. He's eating all by himself."

"Poor old duck. He was the most boring professor we had," Brenda said.

"We should say hello to him."

"Oh, Sofia."

"I'm serious. Coming with me?"

"Not bloody likely."

"You know, Brenda, sometimes you can be a real wet blanket."

Sofia got up and walked over to the professor's table. His eyes lit up. She didn't sit down but talked to him for a few minutes before returning to her friends. "He's here on sabbatical. I asked him to have dinner with us tomorrow night."

"You didn't."

"I did. You don't have to come if you don't want."

They paid their bill, sharing it equally in spite of Rick's protests. "I know you're on a limited budget," said Sofia. "So if we're going to hang out together, we go Dutch, okay?"

Rick suggested they go on to a *cave* he knew about a few blocks away. They walked down winding stairs into a darkened cellar, lit only by candles. Two American folk singers, one black and one white, were performing. They both played guitars and sang in close harmony a series of American and French songs: "I am Climbing Jacob's Ladder," "À la Claire Fontaine," "Boll Weevil." The small but enthusiastic audience did not clap at the end of each song but snapped their fingers in appreciation. At the end of the first set, Rick excused himself for a moment.

"He's making a play for you," said Brenda.

"I have other fish to fry."

"Tell me. Are you still keen on that guy you went out with last year at Trinity? Tony?"

"No, I got over him, thank God. He's getting married. He knocked up Tobi Brigham."

"Really? She always seemed so demure."

Sofia shrugged.

Rick returned. "The black guy tried to put the make on me in the can."

"What did you say?"

"Later."

They laughed, ordered more wine, and stayed for the second set. Rick walked them home.

The next night, they met at a much smaller restaurant Sofia had suggested. It turned out Professor Grimshaw didn't know his way around Paris. He had done his graduate work at Laval in Quebec City and had only visited Paris once before, for a brief two weeks, when he was an underpaid lecturer. He had done the museums, but hadn't had the money to splurge on fancy restaurants. He suggested that Sofia order for him.

"It's such a delight running into you. You were my favourite students, you know."

"What about Connie Dalrymple?"

"She was diligent, but she didn't have your panache." This was addressed specifically to Sofia. "Are you enjoying your studies at the Sorbonne?"

"Yes. Particularly the course in French civilization."

"In French? But of course you comprehend the language. When I first went to Laval, I didn't understand half of what the professors said. And I was very isolated. In Quebec, if you're not French-Canadian you're really out of it. I made very few friends."

Sofia felt sorry for Grimshaw. He was obviously a pedantic old bore; she was not surprised he had few friends. He had lived in residence at Trinity, where he ate at the high table and many evenings had tea with another bachelor, a fussy old economist.

"This is delicious." The waiter had brought him a chicken tagine, ordered by Sofia. "I've never really had good food." The food made in Trinity's kitchens was terrible. Her former boyfriend, Tony, had told her that sometimes, when the meal was particularly dire, the undergraduates had stormed into the kitchen and thrown their food at the plate glass wall of the dietitian's office. At Sofia's parents' house the food was excellent. Although her mother never cooked herself, her standards were high. She drew up the menus prepared by their cook.

At a quarter after nine Sofia announced that she had another appointment, but she promised Professor Grimshaw that she would meet him the following Saturday and take him to the *Orangerie* to view paintings by the impressionists. He thanked her profusely and she left him with Brenda. The conversation lagged, but Brenda told him about a skiing trip at Mont Tremblant where she had had drinks with a movie star. Professor Grimshaw expressed his appreciation of the company of these two accomplished young women and offered to walk her back to her rooms.

A few days later Sofia took Mme. Dudevant to lunch with Mavis Gallant. The two women hit it off. Mme. Gallant was thrilled to meet a descendant of a writer in whom she had always been interested. She had thought of writing about her but instead had become involved in a work about the Dreyfus affair, which she was finding difficult to finish. She confessed that it was easiest for her to complete short fiction. She wanted to know whether Sofia had ambitions as a writer. She offered to read any work the young woman might send her.

In the weeks that followed, Sofia and Brenda escorted Professor Grimshaw on various cultural outings, sometimes together, sometimes one at a time: the Musée Rodin, the Cathedral of St. Denis, the Cluny, the Luxembourg Gardens. He was so grateful that they were genuinely touched.

They sometimes had dinner with Rick; occasionally, Brenda dined with him alone. She couldn't resist asking if he'd reconnected with the black folk singer.

"No, did you think I would? You think I'm a faggot?"

"Sofia and I did discuss it at one point."

"You little bitches. Well, I'm going to prove to you I'm not."

"How?"

"Come to my room after supper."

"I don't know ..."

"You're not a virgin, are you?"

"No." In fact Brenda had masturbated one or two of her previous boyfriends, but she had never actually been penetrated. She had to admit she found Rick attractive; he was a bit short, but very handsome. She had thought he was more interested in Sofia than in her. Sofia was the catch. Not only was she attractive and animated, but her family had money. She decided to take Rick up on his offer.

They walked together hand in hand through the crowds of students on the Boulevard St-Germain to the rue du Bac. Together, they climbed to the fourth floor. His room was tiny, papered in a hideous floral pattern. The bed was unmade and the basin filled with dirty water. The floor was strewn with discarded socks and underwear. Rick made no apologies. He immediately started to undress her. He cupped her breasts in his hands and then began to suck on them. Other boys had fondled her, but this was a new experience. Rick pushed her onto the bed and reached up under her skirt. He found her clitoris and began to massage it. She lay back and let him do what he liked.

WHEN BRENDA GOT BACK to their apartment, Sofia was already

in bed. She wanted to tell Sofia about her experience, but something held her back. It wasn't shame. She was actually pleased with herself. She still felt a warm glow. By the time Rick had pushed his penis into her, she was so relaxed that it hardly hurt at all. She realized he must be an experienced lover. She was lucky to have had such a pleasurable initial experience of full-out sex. She climbed under her own covers and lay in bed in a kind of reverie. She knew she wanted to have sex with Rick again.

For the next few weeks, Brenda and Sofia saw little of each other except in class. Brenda had dinner with Rick and went to his little room afterwards. Sofia had dinner several nights a week with Professor Grimshaw, and often came back to their apartment late. Brenda realized she must be seeing somebody else after she said goodnight to the Professor, but she was reluctant to be thought to be prying. They each kept their own counsel.

One night, Sofia took Professor Grimshaw to the *cave* to hear the folk singers. He was a bit intimidated by the place, but felt he was really experiencing Paris under Sofia's tutelage. He remarked to her that they had reversed roles: she was now the teacher and he the eager pupil. She laughed encouragingly and told him he was being fanciful. At the break, the black singer came over to their table. He said her friend had been there the night before with her boyfriend. He was curious about them and interested to learn that they were Canadians. His partner was Québécois; they had met two years ago in New Orleans and had decided to come to

Paris together. Their little *boîte* was doing very well. He was delighted to be introduced to a real professor.

After the second set, Professor Grimshaw said he had something he wanted to say to Sofia. He suggested they go to a café for a *digestif*. They walked together. Professor Grimshaw offered her his arm. They sat at a table outside the Deux Magots. "You don't usually stay out this late, Professor."

"I think it's time you called me Clarence."

"Very well. But you must stop calling me Miss Cheltenham."

"I would like to call you something else." He took a deep breath. Sofia looked at him quizzically. "Mrs. Grimshaw." Her expression changed. "I want you to marry me."

"But Professor Grimshaw …"

"Clarence, please. I know I'm much older than you. But you're very mature."

"Thank you. But …"

"Please let me finish. You may find this hard to credit, but I'm a virgin. I've waited all my life to find someone like you. Intelligent, knowledgeable, thoughtful, considerate. I'm glad I waited. Not that I've had many opportunities."

Sofia imagined he supposed his virginity was a big plus. She was touched, but embarrassed. She hadn't seen this coming. She smiled, not knowing what to say. He interpreted this as encouragement.

"It could work out very nicely. I have two more years before I retire. You are obviously going to become a university teacher. I could go with you wherever you get a position. I have connections at American universities." He beamed at her.

She took a sip of the Grand Marnier he had ordered for her. "I have to admit this comes as a bit of a surprise."

"I didn't mean to spring it on you, but I didn't know how to proceed more tactfully. As I just told you, I'm not very experienced in these matters."

"I'm flattered. I'll have to think about it. I'm going away for a brief holiday in Italy. Can it wait until I come back?"

"Wouldn't you like me to come with you?"

"I'm visiting relatives. My mother's Italian," she lied. "I'm afraid you'd be bored."

"Very well. I will be patient. Let me walk you to your lodging."

Sofia was aware that Clarence was at least two inches shorter than she. As they walked, it became obvious that the idea of holding her hand hadn't occurred to him. At her door she bent her head slightly towards him and waited. He hesitated, then planted a kiss on her cheek. As she mounted the stairs she regretted giving him any encouragement.

Brenda was already wearing her pyjamas. "How was your date with the old goat?"

"He proposed to me."

"How awful."

"I felt so badly. He must have thought I was leading him on. We went to hear those folksingers. The black guy said he'd seen you the night before with Rick. How's that going?"

"Fine." Sofia waited for more details, but they were not forthcoming.

"I'm going to Italy for a few weeks."

"To see relatives?"

"No. I've got this Italian boyfriend."

"I knew you had something going on. Is it serious?"

"I don't know yet. I'll tell you when I get back."

"You wouldn't really consider Professor Grimshaw's proposal?"

"Of course not. But I do feel sorry for him. And a bit responsible. He is kind of a dear. Will you promise me to have dinner with him at least twice while I'm away?"

"Why not just tell him point blank no deal?"

"Too brutal."

"It's not like you to be so soft-hearted."

"I wonder if we could find someone for him."

"Who?"

"I don't know." Sofia climbed into bed and closed her eyes. Brenda looked at her and realized that the discussion was over.

Sofia stayed in Italy longer than anticipated. In their first conversation after her return, Mme. Dudevant inquired about Sofia's boyfriend. Sofia informed her that he had decided to stay in Rome. He was studying to be a medievalist and he had gained admission to a collection housed in the palace of one of the princely families. Mme. Dudevant asked if she would move to Rome to be with him. Sofia replied that she wondered whether he would be able to spend much time with her. He was a serious student; his work came first. Mme. Dudevant smiled and said she was sure Sofia wouldn't want to play second fiddle to a lot of old manuscripts.

The next day, Sofia met Brenda at a little café on Boulevard St-Michel.

"How was Italy?"

"Fantastico."

"And your guy?"

"He's staying in Rome for a bit," Sofia grimaced.

"You'll be going back there?"

"Don't know. What's new with you, Bren?"

"I'm preggers."

"Are you sure?"

Brenda nodded.

"Rick?"

Brenda nodded again.

"Have you told him?"

"I'm afraid to."

"He'll probably be delighted. Most men are. At least initially."

"Suppose he isn't? He's been moody lately. He isn't getting much work from the *Herald-Tribune*."

"This will give him something to take his mind off that. Have you been seeing Professor Grimshaw?"

"Once a week, as promised. He seems a bit down in the mouth. He misses you."

"Poor lamb."

That night, Brenda had dinner with Rick. They had taken to going to cheap restaurants, frequented by truck drivers, near les Halles. Rick said they were some of the best restaurants in Paris. He confessed his cash was running low. Brenda asked if he was thinking of going back to Toronto.

"No. I'm thinking of going to acting school in London. My old man has promised to stake me to a one-year course they have for foreigners. I figure I should take him up on it."

"Would you like me to come with you?"

"I don't know. I think they keep their students pretty busy. There's not much point me doing this if I don't give it my best shot."

"There's something you should know. I'm pregnant."

She looked at him as the colour drained from his face.

"I thought you'd be pleased."

"Well ... it doesn't exactly fit in with my plans."

"You must have known this could happen. There must have been other girls."

"Not that many, actually." His brow wrinkled.

He looked like a fish on a hook, Brenda thought. "What do you want me to do?"

"Let's talk about it tomorrow? Let's go and have a nightcap at the Deux Magots?" He took her hand and they walked along together, crossing the Seine under the sliver of a moon. They drank brandies in silence. Rick walked her home. They kissed on the doorstep. Brenda thought his kiss was more like a brother's than a lover's.

Sofia was propped up in bed reading a book when Brenda returned. She gave her an inquiring look. Brenda lay down on the bed beside her.

"He doesn't want me," she said, trying to sound calm and rational. Her red nose and tears betrayed her.

"Do you want him?"

"He's very good looking."

"I'll grant you that."

"And a very good lover."

"How many lovers have you had?"

Brenda was put off by Sofia's tone. She didn't reply. There was a brief silence.

"Do you want to have the child?" Brenda didn't answer. "If not, you can always have an abortion."

"I'm too scared."

"It's all right if you get a proper doctor. I can arrange that. I've had two."

"You're so matter-of-fact."

"Would you rather I burst into tears, so we could have a good cry together?" She reached out and put her arm around Brenda. Brenda snuggled against her. They slept together in the same bed that night.

Sofia met Professor Grimshaw for dinner at the Brasserie Lipp the next night. "It's where we first met in Paris. So I thought we should mark our anniversary here."

"Does that mean …?"

"I can't marry you. You see, I'm already engaged to a young man back in Toronto. We've known each other since childhood. Our parents are very close friends. I'm sorry, Clarence. I should have told you before. But I wanted to think about it seriously. To enjoy the idea of the possibility. I'm afraid that was very selfish of me." She looked across at his crestfallen face. "You'll always be very dear to me." She reached across and took his small hand in hers. "Cheer up. I've got a surprise guest who's going to join us. Let's order champagne. Would you like that? My treat."

The waiter arrived with the champagne just as Mme. Dudevant made her appearance. Sofia introduced her to Clarence, saying that madame was her best friend in Paris and she was a descendant of George Sand. She knew the professor would be impressed by this, as indeed he was. Nineteenth-century poetry was his specialty. Sofia had thought it strange that this crabbed little man had chosen the rapturous lyrics of Lamartine and Musset, the dark cynicism of Baudelaire, as his particular field.

Clarence questioned Mme. Dudevant about her illustrious ancestor, but proved to know more than she did. She had never visited Nohant, Sand's family estate. He suggested they might visit it together. She confessed that she had been named Loelia after one of Sand's heroines, though she preferred to be called Lolo. After dessert, Sofia excused herself; she had another engagement.

SOFIA ARRANGED FOR BRENDA's abortion and paid for it. When she came out of the operating room Brenda was tearful, but her expression was one of grim determination. The two girls went to a café and had a couple glasses of wine. Brenda had informed Rick of her decision, which he had greeted with evident relief. They had agreed not to see each other again.

At their next conversation, Sofia quizzed Mme. Dudevant about her reaction to Professor Grimshaw. She said she had found him very intelligent. He had asked her to have dinner with him again in a few days. She had thought about it and decided to accept. "Of course, my dear, I realize you planned this whole thing. What a clever little schemer you are. Can one say that? Schemer?" Sofia nodded assent. "And you, *ma petite*. I have something to say to you. Do not throw away your chance for this boy in Rome unless you are very sure. Are you very sure?"

"Not very sure."

"*Eh, bien.*"

Sofia thought about it for several days. At the end of the week she boarded a train for Rome.

BREAKING OUT

When Graham Hiscock learned that his son Tom was engaged to Nancy, the daughter of his partner, he said to his wife, "Thank God I won't have to meet a whole lot of dreadful new people." Graham was a lawyer in a firm that his grandfather had founded. He knew the prominent figures in Toronto's legal and business world and regularly had lunch with them at the Toronto Club. Tom was his youngest son and the darling of his wife Eleanor. He was also, Graham readily conceded, the brightest of his four children. When Tom graduated with high marks from Cranmer College Graham willingly shelled out for him to attend Harvard, where he was convinced Tom would undoubtedly receive an education superior to that afforded by the University of Toronto, as well as make valuable American contacts.

Tom chose Clarke Bull as his best man. They had been classmates at Cranmer, where one of the highlights of their careers had been appearing together in a production of *The Importance of Being Earnest*, Clarke as Cecily, sporting blond curls and a pink organdy frock, and Tom as Miss Prism, with an improbably large bosom. As Tom was six foot three and his Canon Chasuble was four foot nine, they were accounted brilliant comedians. Clarke was thought to be too pretty by half.

The wedding took place the spring Tom graduated from Harvard and was attended by the people who mattered. The reception was held at the York Club and featured cold lobster hors d'oeuvres and Mumm's Champagne. Tom made a graceful speech in response to the toast to the bride, quoting Shakespeare and Robbie Burns; he finished with a toast to the bridesmaids, as was the custom of the day. In response, Clarke rose to deliver an impassioned attack on the spiritual impoverishment of the Toronto upper middle class, intended to insult the assembled guests. He succeeded. The mother of the bride booed him loudly. Others followed her example. Tom was amused, but managed to keep a straight face. He had always admired his friend's outrageousness and wished he had the courage to emulate it.

Clarke didn't apologize. "I simply couldn't resist when I looked across the room at all those smug faces, Cocky." Clarke had coined this nickname for his friend, a play on his last name. Tom riposted by calling Clarke "Ballsy," a tribute to the pair of low-hanging testicles of which Clarke was inordinately proud. At school, Tom had often observed Clarke in the showers and admired his friend's perfectly proportioned body, which he envied even though Clarke was a good seven inches shorter than Tom.

Tom had a serious talk with his father, who had assumed his son would go into the family firm. Graham grudgingly accepted the boy's decision to accept a position as a university teacher rather than become the brilliant litigator he believed his son was sure to have been. Graham was suspicious of professors of English, many of whom he thought were probably fairies, but at least Tom was safely married to a nice young woman. Following their honeymoon in Barbados, Graham and Nancy's father bought the couple an Edwardian house in south Rosedale. To show their bohemian tastes Tom and Nancy painted the exterior a vibrant shade of yellow, almost chartreuse. The living room contained no chairs or tables but many cushions spread out on an antique Turkish kilim. On the walls they hung colourful canvases created by members of Painters Eleven.

Three weeks before Christmas they gave a party. The invitees were asked to wear "groovy garb" and were sent out on a scavenger hunt. The clues were esoteric and depended on a knowledge of certain fashionable shops, the addresses of various artists, and an insider's knowledge of the internal workings of the university. To Tom's surprise his father, who was partnered with a female CBC producer, won first prize.

While Tom gave lectures on Donne and the metaphysical poets at University College, Nancy worked as an editor with a prominent Canadian publisher. Three months after their wedding she discovered she was pregnant and two days before their first anniversary she was delivered of identical twin boys. Her father paid for her to have a live-in nursemaid. Graham hired a cook — he had discovered, after having dined with the young couple, that Nancy had limited culinary skills and, further, Tom had confided to his father that he actually did most of the cooking. A more than capable Jamaican woman soon took charge of the couple's kitchen. Tom protested, but Graham insisted on the importance of satisfying "the inner man."

Nancy's delivery had been complicated and she showed little interest in sexual activity in the months immediately following the twins' birth. She was absorbed with breastfeeding and the proper diet for the twins, who proved to have severe allergies. Tom spent more time with his students — particularly a bright and attractive Eurasian youth named Sonny Morris, the son of a Canadian diplomat and his Indonesian wife. After exams the two travelled together to Bali and returned with a collection of batiks and carved wooden figures, including a large statue of Hanuman, the monkey god, which Tom installed in his study. Hanuman was said to be a great lover of stories. Tom decided a year later to start a small publishing house with Sonny as a junior editor, working under Nancy's supervision. They named it House of Hanuman and published novels and poetry collections by young and as-yet-unknown writers, one or two of whom would eventually become quite famous.

Clarke returned to Toronto after three years in Paris studying art history at the Sorbonne. He had married a fellow student, a Canadian girl, Wendy Fischer, who was the daughter of a successful brewer and consequently an heiress. Clarke boasted she did not come from old money but rather big money. He took up an appointment as a junior curator at the Royal Ontario Museum. He and Wendy moved into a large house in Forest Hill, where they entertained lavishly. Claremont House, as they named it, was furnished with early French-Canadian armoires, chairs, and cabinets, some of them extravagantly painted in wildly contrasting colours. It was decorated with a series of weathercocks and paintings by Joseph Légaré. Tom and Nancy were frequent guests, as were the President of the University, the Bishop of Toronto, the editor of *The Globe and Mail*, and the president of the CBC. Clarke began writing articles for the newspaper; he was soon appointed an assistant professor in the history department and began appearing as a commentator on television. He also was appointed Rector's Warden at the cathedral.

In the early autumn, Graham was diagnosed with pancreatic cancer. Tom went to see him in St. Michael's Hospital. He had brought his father a cashmere sweater to wear on the golf course in Florida. Graham thanked him but said, "Keep it for yourself. I know I've had it."

"We're all rooting for you."

"Don't waste your breath. You know, Tom, you haven't turned out as badly as I feared. I'm counting on you to look after your mother. You know you're her favourite. I hope you won't do anything she'd be ashamed of."

"I don't know what you mean."

"I think you do. There's a bottle of whisky in my nightstand. Just pour me two fingers and have some yourself."

They drank together for the last time.

Tom was shaken by his father's death, but at the same time relieved. He came out from under the cloud of disapproval, which he felt had hung over his head almost since his birth. He felt freed from the strictures imposed by his class, free to be himself, free at last to follow his own bent.

The next summer, Clarke took off for Quebec City, leaving his wife and infant son behind. He stayed in the flat of a cousin of Tom's in the lower town. He explored the ancient buildings of the city and also its low life. He returned to Toronto with the manuscript of a novel, *The Plains of Abraham*, whose hero, Rupert Waddington, was an obvious stand-in for Clarke himself. What was bound to catch the reader's attention were Rupert's encounters with male hustlers — one of which took place behind the high altar in the cathedral — and the identification of the ecstasy of sexual climax with the spiritual communion of the Eucharist. The text was shot through with such pronouncements as "I can't think with my balls cut off. There's no substitute for a thoughtful pair of balls."

He submitted his novel to Tom's press and Tom was keen to publish it, but Nancy voiced a strenuous objection. "I thought we were interested in promising work of literary quality, not pornographic trash." Tom, as president of Hanuman, overruled her decision. The novel quickly became the talk of Toronto.

TOM'S MOTHER INVITED HIM to lunch at her new apartment at Oaklands. "I do hope you know what you're doing, Tom," she said over coffee. "Publishing that dreadful novel of Clarke's. I can imagine what your father would have thought of it."

"He's one of my oldest friends, Mother."

"That's no excuse. Friendship should not override common decency."

A few weeks later, Wendy's parents decided to give a lavish party for their daughter in their mansion on Old Post Road. Champagne flowed; shrimp and lobster canapés were proffered in abundance by a staff of handsome waiters; two orchestras played for dancing in a huge marquee spread over the lawn; perfume was wafted through the night air by several young women squirting atomizers at the guests.

It was whispered that the purpose of the fête was to show that Clarke and Wendy were still together. But Clarke was nowhere in evidence and Wendy danced repeatedly with a former beau. At the height of the revelry, four very tall and elegant women, two of them black, took over the centre of the dance floor and began to gyrate provocatively. It became apparent they were transvestites. They conveyed greetings from Clarke. Tom, who was a bit tipsy, danced with one of the girls, his long legs and arms flailing awkwardly out of sync with the beat of the music. The guests had already begun to disperse, mumbling that Clarke and Wendy's marriage was obviously on the rocks.

ON THE WAY HOME Nancy, who was driving their Mercedes, commented, "You made quite a spectacle of yourself. How long have you known about Clarke's homosexual tendencies?"

"Quite a while now."

"Were you ever lovers?"

Tom hesitated. "Once at school. Long ago. We didn't do anything much."

"Not more recently? When you went to visit him in Quebec, for instance?"

"No."

"What about Sonny? I've sometimes wondered ..."

"It's not serious," said Tom.

"Do you consider our marriage serious?"

"Don't get upset, Nancy. It doesn't matter."

"It matters to me." She drove on in silence.

When they reached their house in Rosedale, Tom poured himself a stiff whisky and sat in the darkened living room, listening to a recording of a Mozart piano sonata. When he went upstairs he found that Nancy had locked their bedroom door. Tom had wanted to talk to Nancy about his newfound sense of freedom, but something had been holding him back. A sense that she wouldn't understand, that she would be shocked by the callowness of his reaction to his father's death. His intuition had proved accurate. Sitting on the floor of the hall outside the bedroom door, he realized that his vaunted sense of freedom had come up against the brick wall of family convention. He was forced to acknowledge his need to retain the approval of his mother and his wife. His father's shadow was not so easily dismissed as he had imagined.

A FEW WEEKS LATER, Tom took Clarke to lunch at the University Club. He had just learned that Clarke had insulted the new director of the Museum and had been fired on the spot.

"What are you going to do now?"

"Don't worry, Cocky. I have an offer from the Smithsonian."

"You'll take it, of course."

"I don't know. I can't imagine becoming an American."

"What about Wendy?"

"What about her?"

"I hear she's suing for divorce."

"Let her sue. I have nothing she wants."

"The rumour is you've run through her fortune."

"She's had the advantage of my superior taste. She should have the grace to be grateful."

"And your son?"

"She's welcome to him. Nasty little beast. How are you getting along with Nancy?"

"We're in therapy."

"You should have the balls to break free."

"I don't know that I want to."

"I'm disappointed in you, Cocky. You're not fulfilling your early promise."

"Unlike you?"

"I need to be true to the integrity of my vision."

Tom could think of no suitable response. In silence, the two old friends tucked into their rare roast beef sandwiches and demolished a bottle of Nuits-St-Georges.

A FEW WEEKS LATER, Clarke went to address the students at his old school Cranmer, where his brother Jonathan was now headmaster. His attack on the establishment was expected and welcomed by many of the students. Less expected was his seduction of a red-headed fifteen-year-old boy, with whom he absconded the following morning. The two of them flew to Mexico where they holed up in a friend's villa. Clarke sent Tom a note: *I have reached the point at which I have to live out my crisis. My crisis is a spiritual one. I'm homosexual, but not gay. It is not the homosexual I want, it is the sentient man. A new kind of man. I think you are secretly looking for the same thing. Why don't you and Sonny join us in Oaxaca?*

Tom didn't respond, though for the rest of his life a part of him would wish he had.

ANGEL CAKE

Morgan picked up his phone and growled into the mouthpiece irritably, "Yes?" He had given his unlisted phone number to very few people and it was six o'clock in the morning. An English voice informed him that it was Claridge's Hotel in London calling on behalf of his purported friend Mr. de Travers, who had run up a bill of some one-hundred-and-seventy-three pounds, which he was unable to pay. He had suggested that his Canadian godfather, Morgan Bedford, might agree to pay it. Reluctantly, Morgan got out of bed, found his wallet, and gave the caller his Visa number authorizing him to charge the card for the sum of up to two hundred pounds.

He returned to bed and fell back to sleep. He was awakened again three quarters of an hour later by the same voice icily informing him that Mr. de Travers had proceeded to the bar where he had run up a bill for the remaining twenty-three pounds and then called a cab. When it arrived he had lifted the silk hat of the doorman, placed it on his head, and ridden away. Morgan declined to pay the cost of the purloined headgear and hung up.

Morgan was not in fact Marq's godfather, but had been his teacher in a journalism course at Ryerson. In spite of his provocative and often impudent questions in class, Morgan had realized early on that Mark Travers was a clever and stylish writer — although he could neither spell nor punctuate. Morgan had a weakness for entertaining young people; he took Mark under his wing. Mark became the son Morgan never had. He found the "q" and the "de" — affectations first adopted on a trip to France — amusing if a bit ridiculous, but when they took a cruise in the Mediterranean together, a steward accosted them: *"M. le Marquis, suivez-moi, s'il vous plait."* He took them to an upper deck, where he installed them in a first-class cabin. Who knew that as late as 1980 perceived aristocratic lineage could accrue such benefits? After this, the affectation became permanent.

Morgan set his precocious student up with the editor of two magazines for which he wrote on a regular basis. He let Marq move into the spare bedroom in his condo for several months after he had had a particularly nasty squabble with his mother. Morgan and Marq began to write the book for a mini-musical about a young singer named Angel Cake and her rise to stardom. It was to be a vehicle for Marq's girlfriend, Angie, who played jazz piano and had a good voice. Morgan had persuaded a friend to compose four tunes for the lyrics he had penned. They filled out the score with standards from Rodgers and Hart and Cole Porter.

Marq's refuge with Morgan ended the night Morgan came home to find Marq and a street hustler making out on his prized Royal Sarouk carpet. He stood and watched while the young man dressed hastily and then demanded payment. Morgan had to get out his wallet and hand over eighty dollars before the hustler would leave. Marq offered no apology. Morgan told him he would have to get out in the morning.

A FEW DAYS AFTER the midnight phone call, Morgan heard from Angie, who informed him that Marq was back in Toronto. She suggested that the three of them meet for a drink and dinner at Arlequin, a restaurant conveniently situated on Avenue Road a few blocks north of his condo. Morgan was fond of Angie, but he was unsure what her relationship to Marq was at the moment. After the incident with the hustler, Marq had taken off for Europe where he had been for the past three months.

Morgan and Angie nursed their white wine spritzers for almost an hour at Arlequin before Marq made his entrance, wearing a curly blond wig that might have been left over from a Restoration comedy, and dressed in black with a flowered, long-fringed Spanish shawl which he had draped around his shoulders. He kissed Angie and Morgan on both cheeks, "in the French manner." The waiter arrived and poured him a glass of water, which he tasted and then sent back to the kitchen, claiming it was stale. The waiter brought a bottle of

Perrier. Marq asked for a fresh lime. Then he turned to Angie. "Are you still game to do our little show?"

"We're already two weeks into rehearsal. It's my day off."

"You started without me?"

"You knew we were going to."

Morgan changed the subject. "I thought you might like to see the poster."

"Why is your name ahead of mine?"

"It's alphabetical. Bedford before Travers."

"It will have to be redone. My new pen name is Aaron Aardvark." Marq ordered a bottle of Dom Pérignon. When informed the restaurant didn't carry it, he agreed to accept the "decidedly inferior" Veuve Clicquot. He ordered a green salad to be followed by a lobster soufflé, though the latter was not on the menu. After an uncomfortable silence, during which the champagne was brought to the table and poured into a tall flute for Marq, he proceeded to tell Angie and Morgan how the Spanish brandy distiller Pedro Domecq had entertained him for a weekend at his villa in Marbella, where he had seduced a young condesa. Morgan and Angie finished their spritzers and gave each other a long look of incredulity.

Interrupted by the arrival of the salad, Marq looked at it balefully. He took one bite and summoned the waiter. "This is inedible. Take it away. Bring me a Boston lettuce, fresh basil, extra-virgin olive oil, raspberry vinegar, dry mustard, salt and pepper and call the chef. I will show him how to make a green salad."

The waiter returned to the kitchen with the rejected salad.

Marq looked at Angie. "I'm crashing at the parents', but I'm hoping to move in with you tonight. I want to avoid another donnybrook with the old witch."

"I'm afraid that won't work, Marq. I've got a new boyfriend."

"You ungrateful little whore." Marq rose to his feet and walked away. "Bitch, bitch, bitch," he screamed, slamming the door behind him.

Silence descended on the restaurant. The waiter returned to the table. "We value you as a customer, Mr. Bedford, but you are never to bring that young man to this restaurant again. What shall I do with the champagne?"

"Leave it and bring two more glasses."

"Very good, sir." Morgan and Angie waited until the waiter had come back with two flutes, which he filled with champagne. Morgan raised his glass in a toast. "Angel Cake." Their glasses clinked.

"He should see a doctor."

"I'll talk to him about it."

MARQ TURNED UP AT Morgan's condo two nights later at midnight with a hockey bag full of clothes, which he dropped just inside the door. He doffed his wig, revealing a completely shaved head, walked to Morgan's bar, and poured himself a tumbler of Glenfiddich. He headed for the stereo, where he put on an album of Nina Simone and turned the volume up full. "The old witch has picked a fight about my bringing home a bag of dirty laundry for her to wash. I told her I was checking out and brought it to you." He walked back to the hockey bag and opened the zipper, held it up, and dumped a pile of dirty shirts, socks, and underwear on the floor. He was starting to go through it when Morgan got up and turned the sound off.

"Hey, I need that. I'm depressed."

"It's midnight."

"So what?"

"Have you thought about seeing a doctor?"

"Have you got anything to eat?"

Marq went into the kitchen and began to take things out of the refrigerator. He cut up some onions, mushrooms, and red peppers and then broke six eggs into the frying pan.

"I've taken charge of my own medical condition."

"Since when?"

"Since before I went to Spain."

Morgan wondered if Marq was still taking his prescribed lithium, but decided this was not the moment to ask. He was aware Marq had been promiscuous when he was dating Angie. He had frequented the bathhouses and picked up people in the streets. Angie knew it too, but seemed willing to accept it. Morgan supposed she loved Marq in spite of his unpredictable behaviour. Once Marq had borrowed Morgan's car without permission and driven with Angie out to the Cherry Street spit. They had made love in the moonlight on the beach, then Marq had picked up a young man and driven off with him, leaving Angie to make her own way home. He was arrested shortly after for driving without a licence. Morgan had had to go to the police station and bail him out — as well as pay the towing charges.

Marq was separating his dirty laundry into two piles, one that he intended to keep, the other to go to what he referred to as "The Crumpled Spivs," although the organization had changed its name to Goodwill. He was torn as to whether to part with a gold silk jacket, finally deciding it was "too sixties." He offered it to Morgan who declined and went to bed.

THE NEXT DAY, WHEN Marq showed up at rehearsal at eleven thirty, the cast of *Angel Cake* were on a break. Marq was wearing black silk pyjamas Morgan recognized had been filched from his dresser. After a short coughing fit, Marq announced, "I've decided we should scrap those stupid tunes you wrote the lyrics for, Morgan. The music is derivative. We could replace them with new lyrics I've written for a series we can call *Herb Hits*: 'Thyme on my Hands,' 'My Rosemary, I Love You,' 'I'll Never Forget Sweet Marjoram,' 'You're My Dill' …"

"You're joking." Todd, the director, was incredulous, but his voice was controlled. He had been forewarned Marq might make trouble.

"*Au contraire*. We will retitle the show *The Stink of Love*."

Morgan was not amused. He had invested a good deal of time and effort, not to mention some of his own money, in developing and producing *Angel Cake*. Marq had contributed two or three amusing scenes, but had left it to Morgan to stitch the whole thing together. Now he was sharply disparaging his efforts. Morgan was sensitive to criticism of his work and resented Marq's high-handed and capricious attitude.

"Where's Angie?" asked Marq.

"She's in the washroom. She's not feeling well," Morgan answered.

"Look, we've been rehearsing those numbers for two weeks. We're not going to change now, six days before opening," Todd said, the exasperation notable in his voice.

"We'll see about that."

Angie came out of the washroom. She looked a bit pale, but said she was ready to go back to work. She eyed Marq with concern. "You don't look too great."

"Neither do you. In fact you look ghastly. You should go home and get some sleep, if you're planning to be in my show."

Todd walked over to Marq. He was a head taller and considerably more muscular. "You're going to leave this building now."

Marq spat in his face. Todd grabbed him by the collar and dragged him to the door. "You're just lucky I'm not throwing you down the stairs. You are not welcome at any more rehearsals."

"You'll be hearing from my lawyers."

Two days later Todd received a phone call from Marq, informing him that his lawyers had advised him to withdraw permission to use any part of his work on the script of *Angel Cake*. He would be receiving written notice to cease and desist within forty-eight hours. Todd consulted Morgan, pointing out that they couldn't do a complete rewrite in two or three days and certainly couldn't afford a lawsuit. Morgan thought it unlikely that Marq had any money to hire a lawyer in the first place.

"There's always one lawyer out there who's willing to take on any case, however preposterous."

"I'll talk to him."

But Marq was not at Morgan's condo. He had left a note saying he was flying to Rome the next day. Morgan got in touch with Marq's mother, who said she had no idea where her son was. He then went to a hustlers' pick-up bar on Yonge Street, where he thought he remembered Marq used to hang out. Marq was sitting at the bar beside a martini glass. Morgan expected to be met with hostility, but instead Marq gave him an affable if somewhat bleary grin. "Good to see you. You can pick up my tab."

Morgan sat down on the stool next to Marq, who reached over and put his arm around Morgan's shoulder. "I'm sorry about the show. But my lawyers insisted."

"I'm sorry too. For Angie's sake."

"She betrayed me. Everyone's betrayed me."

"I don't think I've betrayed you."

Marq started to cry. "You've been like a father to me." His sobs bordered on hysteria. Morgan was touched, in spite of the fact that he had decided he'd put up with enough of Marq's nonsense. "I'll have another martini." The bartender looked at Marq stonily.

"It's all right. I'll see he gets home." Morgan got out his wallet and paid Marq's bill, then walked him to the door and helped him into a cab.

Back at the condo Morgan sat in a chair while Marq got undressed. He noticed that Marq had lost weight. His body showed several bruises and his underpants were stained. Marq grinned at him. "Mr. Skinnyshanks."

"I want you to do something for me."

"What?"

"I want you to bring your lawyer to a meeting with me and Todd tomorrow at five o'clock at The Pilot Tavern, so we can straighten things out."

"Okay. But you'll have to meet my terms. Seventy per cent of the gross and my name above the title."

"Which name?"

But Marq didn't answer. He had passed out. Morgan put his arm under Marq's shoulder and carried him into the spare bedroom.

THE NEXT DAY, ON Morgan's advice, they rehearsed as usual. At five o'clock he and Todd arrived at The Pilot. They ordered a couple of beers and waited for an hour. There was no sign of Marq or his lawyers.

Morgan went home. The television was on and there was an empty bottle of whisky on the coffee table in front of it. Morgan poured himself a shot of Macallan from a fresh bottle and turned the television off.

The phone rang. "Morgan."

"We waited an hour for you."

"I'm in the Women's College Hospital. I'm scared. Please come."

Morgan took a cab to the hospital. After a wait of twenty minutes he was shown into a room where Marq was lying in bed, hooked up to intravenous, a machine that seemed to be monitoring his heartbeat, and an oxygen tank. He turned to Morgan with a sad little smile. "I've had a heart attack."

Morgan took his hand and held it. Marq closed his eyes.

After about half an hour, Marq let go of his hand. Morgan went to the payphone and dialled Angie's number. He asked her to come to the hospital as soon as she could. He went back to Marq's room and sat in silence. An hour later, Angie appeared in the doorway. She entered and sat on the edge of Marq's bed. He opened his eyes. "What are you doing here? I suppose Morgan called you. Well, he's not running my life anymore. Nobody is." He lay back, breathing heavily, his eyes closed.

Suddenly Marq had a violent coughing fit and brought up a quantity of yellow phlegm streaked with blood. Angie wiped it up with Kleenex. Marq tried to sit up but sank back on his pillow. He opened his eyes and looked straight at Angie. "I always loved you best. Now clear out of here, both of you."

Morgan stood over his bed. "Marq …"

Marq had another coughing fit.

"You heard me. Out."

His voice was feeble. They left.

Back at the condo, Morgan and Angie poured themselves shots from the bottle of Macallan.

"Do you think he's faking?"

"About the heart attack or the lawyers?"

"Maybe both?" Tears streamed down Angie's cheeks. Morgan put his arms around her before he put her in a cab. He realized to his surprise that at this point he felt more sympathy for her than he did for Marq.

THE NEXT MORNING, MORGAN received a phone call from Marq's mother informing him that Marq had died at five o'clock that morning.

Angel Cake opened as planned to a full house, mostly friends and well-wishers. Morgan sat at the back of the small theatre as Angie's clear soprano carried his lyrics out over the audience.

Now it's plain the game is done
And in the end, my friend,
It wasn't that much fun
I'm wiser now, I see it's true
The one who understood the game was you.

Morgan hadn't written the words thinking of Marq, but now his eyes were moist. He wished Marq had been there to share in the realization of their joint endeavour. Had it been worthwhile putting up with Marq's impossible shenanigans in the last month to achieve this?

Morgan made a brief showing at the reception after the show. He kissed Angie and congratulated her, then left, returning to his condo. He poured himself a healthy shot of Macallan and turned on the stereo. The record of Nina Simone was still on the turntable. Her smoky voice filled the room as she intoned the bittersweet lyrics of "Solitaire."

Morgan had not played his hand carelessly. On the contrary, he had been if anything too cautious. Over the years he had been attracted to a number of his students, of both sexes. He had sometimes come close to making a pass at one of them. He had thought about having sex with Marq when they shared a cabin on their Mediterranean cruise, but he had set himself a strict prohibition against sex with his students. Not that many of his colleagues had similar qualms. Morgan told himself he had put up with Marq's behaviour because right up to the end he had lived full out. He had dared to be outrageous. It was Marq's sheer boldness and extravagance that he admired and envied, but could never quite bring himself to emulate.

THE MATING GAME

Dr. Yi Hsio-ling set out for the airport, dressed in her new brown shantung silk suit, with an ancient necklace of amber and silver that had belonged to her mother. She had long ago realized she was no beauty, but it was important to her to make the most of her appearance. Her suits were made by a first-class tailor. She bought shoes from Papagallo when she went to Europe every second summer. She always wore suits, sometimes with pants, sometimes with skirts — but never slit up the side to her thigh. She didn't care to look like Suzie Wong.

She was on her way to meet Roderick Burke, her former colleague at the University of Toronto, who was visiting Hong Kong for the first time. She had invited him several times before, as long ago as 1972, but only when he had finished his book on Simone Martini did he consent to come for a ten-day visit, and then only because he wanted to consult some documents he believed were lodged in Beijing, relating to early Sino-European trade routes. Ling had made some preliminary researches and had used her contacts with the authorities in mainland China to open doors for him. Her interest in Roddy was not primarily scholarly.

He was one of the last off the plane, and when he finally appeared with three large suitcases, looking decidedly flustered, she stepped forward and quickly engaged a porter. She would have thought he'd have learned to travel more efficiently by now. At fifty-six, surely he should have realized he didn't need so many suitcases. There were laundries and dry cleaners in Hong Kong.

Once Roddy's bags were stowed in the trunk of her car, Dr. Yi Hsio-ling took the wheel and they proceeded back into the city. Roddy was impressed by the view of the harbour. Ling pointed out some of the highlights of the city as they mounted The Peak in her standard shift BMW. Roddy complimented her on her skills as a driver as she negotiated the hairpin turns of the mountain on their way to a tall apartment building. Once inside her spacious apartment, furnished as he would have expected with restrained good taste, Roddy stood looking out over the harbour across to Kowloon while Hsio-ling prepared green tea and set out little sesame honey cakes she had baked that morning. Roddy was jet-lagged after fourteen hours in the air and hoped for a quiet evening at home.

"We're going to dinner at the Peninsula," she announced. "I want you to meet my friend Marcus. He's a dealer in

Oriental antiques in New York. A very amusing fellow. He always entertains his friends when he comes here. It'll be a good introduction for you to one level of Hong Kong society. You can have a short snooze before you get dressed."

Roddy was well aware that Ling's plans, once formulated, were not to be challenged. Her determination had elevated her to the position of Curator of Chinese Antiquities at the Royal Ontario Museum. It had also led to her downfall when she had insisted on being given three additional galleries so she could display the collection properly. "After all, it's the most important thing this museum has. It's what people come to see, not those moth-eaten grizzly bears and tigers." But children liked the bears and tigers; the members of the Museum's board voted down her request. She resigned in protest. The museum's director didn't know where she thought she would find a comparable post. But within two months Ling was offered a full professorship at the University of Hong Kong, with a considerably higher salary.

Roddy emerged from his bedroom at six-thirty in a smart tropical suit and a flamboyant tie. He and Ling took the elevator to the underground garage and got into Ling's car.

"I see you've faced up to the fact you need glasses."

"Only for reading fine print," replied Roddy, hastily removing them and stowing them in his breast pocket.

"And you've decided to become a blond. Are you having more fun?"

Roddy said nothing, but shrugged and flashed Ling a self-deprecating grin. He was used to her tart tongue. As he had become familiar with other Asians he had come to think of it as an aspect of their culture. On first acquaintance they seemed excessively polite; but, once he got to know them well, they were often brutally frank. One of his students, after he had treated him to dinner accompanied by an excellent bottle of wine, had said, "You not so young I think." Another had commented on his erratic driving. In both cases he had pretended not to hear, but in fact had been stung by their remarks.

"I suppose you think it makes you look younger, but in fact it emphasizes the lines on your forehead and around your eyes."

"Don't most middle-aged Chinese dye their hair?"

"Not I. I think grey hair suits me."

They pulled up in front of the hotel, where Ling handed the car keys to a valet. Two bellboys in tight white bumfreezer jackets and little round white caps opened the doors for them. They made their way up to a room filled with people standing, drinks in hand. The table was set for sixteen. Ling introduced Roddy to their host, Marcus, a handsome man in his early forties with a shock of chestnut hair hanging over his forehead.

"I've heard about you. Not just from Ling. I have this friend who's a curator at the Met who says you know more about Italian painting in the *Trecento* than anyone else in North America, with the possible exception of himself. What a wonderful tie."

"It was a gift. I hesitated, wondering if it might be a soupçon too outré."

"Roddy's nothing if not cautious."

"It's to die for. Come and meet some of my guests."

Roddy was introduced to a British brigadier, a female Irish novelist, an American journalist, and two Roman sisters, one a contessa, who were in town to buy jade. The sisters spoke little English, but he charmed them with his fluent command of their language, spoken in his elegant Tuscan accent. He found himself seated between them at dinner; after the soup, a spicy clear broth, and before the veal paillard, the older sister, who ran an antique shop in a little street near the Pantheon, invited him to visit her at her little beach house on Stromboli.

Over dessert there was a heated discussion about "pilling" — a particular quality that sometimes showed up in the glaze of late Ming pottery and was much prized by certain collectors. Marcus had found a particularly fine specimen earlier in the day and he knew who would buy it in New York for whatever price he cared to ask.

"Do you just find these things somewhere in the back of all those little shops crowded with Buddhas and whatnot?" asked the novelist.

"Good God, no. People come to me. I have a certain reputation." Marcus's smile almost masked his condescension. "Would you like to come and watch me buy a few pieces tomorrow morning?"

"I work in the mornings." She bristled slightly. She had picked up on his tone.

Roddy plunged in to ease the tension. "I'd love to observe."

"Splendid. You have to promise not to say a word."

"Of course."

The brigadier offered a story about how he had been given a silver bowl by some nawab in India before Independence that had fetched over five hundred pounds at Sotheby's.

The party broke up early. Marcus laid a hand on Roddy's shoulder. "Ten o'clock is not too early for you?"

"No, of course not."

"Excellent. Come to my suite here in the hotel. Room 710."

When they got home, Ling poured them each a generous glass of neat Scotch. "You made a hit with Marcus. He has a marvellous apartment on Fifth Avenue right across from the Met."

"How convenient."

"Indeed. I have to lecture tomorrow morning. Just call a cab. The number's there by the telephone. Would you like to give a lecture to one of my classes?"

"I'd be flattered."

"Thursday afternoon, then. Two o'clock." She handed him a spare key. "I'll be gone all day tomorrow, but we'll meet here for drinks, say around five-thirty?"

Roddy undressed without finishing his unpacking and two minutes after his head hit the pillow he was sound asleep.

The next morning he turned up on time at the Peninsula. Marcus greeted him cheerily and offered him croissants and coffee. He sat in a comfortable wing chair and the session began. A steady stream of people were ushered in by a bell-boy. They were all Chinese, but varied in age, sex, and dress:

old women in baggy traditional trousers, young men wearing knock-offs of smart Italian clothes, young women got up to look sexy in short skirts and sheer pantyhose, businessmen in suits with vests, labourers in jeans and T-shirts. They all carried packages, some elaborately wrapped, some in shopping bags, many just bundled up in old newspapers. The parcels were opened and the contents set on a table before Marcus. He examined each piece carefully, then handed it back or named a price in Cantonese. There was very little haggling. The would-be sellers looked on impassively and either rewrapped their treasures and bore them away or pocketed the bills they received and departed. The whole proceeding took just over two hours. At its end, Marcus looked at the eleven pieces of porcelain sitting on the table and smiled across at Roddy.

"As usual most of the stuff they brought in was junk, although these two Ming vases are quite good and that export bowl, though it's only late nineteenth century, is very pretty. Those two little dishes are genuine Sung. I have a client in New York who will take them sight unseen — that's twenty thousand right there. That pays for this trip. Let's go to lunch."

Marcus led Roddy to a noisy restaurant and ordered from the dim sum trolleys a number of delectable dishes Roddy hadn't tasted before, in spite of the fact that he had often had lunch in Toronto's better Chinese restaurants with Ling. Marcus smiled at him.

"This is your first trip to Hong Kong?"

"Yes. I've been meaning to come for some years, but ..."

"So you don't know your way around? Well. Of course Ling knows the territory better than I do, but there may be one or two places of interest to you that she doesn't know about. I take it we are of the same persuasion?"

Roddy twigged instantly, but wasn't sure what was coming next. He merely turned his head slightly towards Marcus.

"Oh, don't worry, you're not my type. But I thought you might like to know there's a sauna in a third-rate hotel about two blocks from here. It's a bit grotty but it might be worth a visit. There's a proper bathhouse in Kowloon where people go to meet. It closes at ten. They lock the doors and anyone who wants to stay the night can have a high old time until they unlock them again at seven the next morning."

"What happens if someone has a heart attack?"

"I suppose that's just the risk you take. But, as we used to say, 'What a way to go.' I've written down the addresses on the back of my card. Good hunting."

After lunch, Roddy strolled through the streets looking in shop windows. He knew perfectly well he would end up in the sauna before the afternoon was over. He went in, got a locker, undressed, wrapped a towel around himself, and headed into the steam room. There was only one other customer, a fat middle-aged man who nodded to him. Roddy sat, bored but enjoying the steam. The fat man left. He decided to stay another five minutes and started counting to three hundred.

At two hundred and twenty-six, the door opened and in

came a tall, thin Chinese boy with long hair tied in a ponytail. He was muscular but not over-developed, with broad shoulders over which he had draped his towel and a tiny waist around which he wore a leather belt. He had very pronounced eyebrows and these gave him a particularly exotic appearance. He sat close to Roddy and eyed him with an appraising candour. "I give very good massage," he said after a moment.

"Here?" Roddy asked.

"Not here. You have place?"

Roddy remembered that Ling had said she would be out all day. He gave the boy a long look and said, "Yes."

"We go?"

Roddy nodded. They dried themselves, got into their clothes, hailed a cab and were back at Ling's apartment within twenty minutes.

"Would you like tea?" Roddy asked.

"After," said the boy as he shed his jeans and T-shirt. Roddy lay on his belly and the naked boy kneeled astride him. Roddy could feel his soft balls brushing against his backside. Two hours later they sat naked in Ling's living room drinking green tea as the boy eyed the drawings on the walls with interest. Roddy tingled with satisfaction. He had come three times and the boy twice.

"Good art."

"They belong to my friend."

"Good taste. I must go now."

"Can I see you again?"

"Yes. Friday afternoon."

He sat looking expectantly at Roddy. Roddy went into the bedroom and came back with fifty American dollars. The boy looked at it and said, "Thank you." He seemed satisfied. Roddy wondered if he'd overpaid him. The boy tucked the money into his pocket and was gone. Roddy looked out the window and down into the street. He expected to see the boy walk away, but there was no sign of him. Did he have another assignation somewhere nearby, possibly even in the same building? He dismissed the question and gazed across the harbour as the light started to wane.

RODDY OFFERED TO TAKE Ling to dinner, hoping she would suggest a wonderful Chinese restaurant. Instead she opted for the Mandarin Hotel, which she said was the only place a decent steak could be had. She sat with a double Scotch, cigarette in hand.

"I have a proposition for you. How would you like to come here for three years as a visiting professor?"

"To teach European art history?"

"European history: art, politics, economics. You know enough to do it. You'd have to teach undergraduates, but the students here are much keener than the ones in North America. They really want to learn and by the time they get to us they have excellent work habits. You'd have graduate students as well."

"The salary?"

"They'd more than match what you're getting now. You

know you could get a leave of absence from good old U of T. As long as they've got your salary to play with while you're gone, they'll agree to just about anything. You've got tenure. They can't get rid of you."

"You've got it all figured out."

"I wouldn't have brought it up otherwise. I do care about you, you know."

Roddy smiled, at a loss as to how to respond. How much was she implying? He looked into her face, but couldn't help thinking she looked like a little russet apple that had made it through the winter.

"Think about it, will you? You've got until you come back from Beijing to make up your mind."

"I'm very flattered."

"So you should be. You wouldn't believe how many people apply for positions here."

"Thanks, Ling."

The meal was excellent. They knew what Ling wanted and provided it. Roddy could imagine how many times she must have sent things back to the kitchen. She had ordered a bottle of Nuits-St-Georges and two brandies, and the bill was formidable — but she was putting him up, never mind the job offer. After scrutinizing it thoroughly, he paid the bill without question.

The next day, Roddy went downtown and walked around the city. He was still tingling with pleasure; his thoughts never strayed far from the afternoon before. In his mind he saw his lover's flat belly and wiry, muscular arms, felt the boy's silky skin against his own and the light brush of his long straight black hair across his chest as the boy bent to suck his nipples. He walked through the market, where old women held up their wares to catch his eye, and along the waterfront where he heard the chatter of sharp high-pitched voices and the clack of the tiles in a dozen games of mah-jong. In the afternoon he found the shop of Ling's tailor and was measured for a silk suit, charcoal grey with patch pockets. He thought of ordering two, but curbed his extravagance.

Home by five, he found Ling had already poured herself a shot of Scotch; he declined to join her, knowing they were going to a Beaujolais Nouveau party at the home of one of her colleagues. It seemed more than a little absurd as an excuse for a party here in Hong Kong, but Ling promised that there would be amusing people in attendance. It proved to be just as mixed a crowd as at Marcus's dinner. Roddy had a pleasant conversation with a young Indian on faculty in the department of literature; the young man admitted that it seemed a bit odd to be teaching English Romantic poetry to a group of Chinese engineering and economic majors.

"I wrote my master's thesis on Wordsworth, but I saw my very first daffodil four years later when I visited Britain," the Indian professor said. "But the best of our students are headed for Oxford or Cambridge, where they'll be expected to know about these things." Roddy asked whether he enjoyed teaching the students in Hong Kong. "They are bright, but not really imaginative. Or, if they are, they don't let it show. They want to give you answers that are correct, not original. There are occasional exceptions."

The voices had become a cacophony as more Beaujolais Nouveau was consumed; the air was blue with cigarette smoke and the temperature seemed to be rising, augmented by an ever increasing number of bodies. Roddy wandered out onto the terrace and looked at the lights flickering across the water. A tall woman with striking snow-white hair came and stood beside him. "You must be Roddy. You match perfectly Ling's description." She had a slight European accent that he couldn't place. "She talks a great deal about you. About the amusing times you spent together in Toronto and how she misses them."

"You don't think she is happy here?"

"I think it is you that she misses."

"She seems to have many friends here."

"Not friends of the heart. She has told you I suppose that the university will invite you to come as a guest?"

"Yes, she has."

"Surely you are tempted? It is something of an honour, even for a scholar of your eminence."

"I don't speak Chinese."

"You could learn. Ling says you are a brilliant linguist."

"I haven't tried to master a new language for over a decade."

"Time for a new challenge. And it would make Ling so happy."

"I'm fond of Ling, but —"

"And she is more than fond of you. You must know that."

Roddy said nothing.

"Think about it. Hong Kong is exciting and vibrant. It is a great jumping-off point for so many fascinating destinations. Beijing, Shanghai, Tokyo, Bangkok, Jakarta."

They were interrupted by their host, who appeared with a bottle to refill their glasses. "It is not a bad year, I think, but not quite up to '81. Would you prefer something else? Whisky? Vodka? No? Come, I want to introduce you to another historian." And he led Roddy back into the room where he exchanged somewhat-empty pleasantries with a rather deaf German.

Roddy finished his glass and looked around for Ling. He was ready to go home, but she was just getting wound up. She was deep in conversation with an American who deplored the idea of growing trade between the U.S. and China, which Ling pronounced inevitable and definitely beneficial to both parties. Roddy stood and listened, contributing little. He was feeling a bit bleary, having drunk more wine than he was accustomed to. When he and Ling left, he was in a state of nervous anxiety all the way home. They arrived without mishap. Upstairs, Ling headed for the whisky bottle. He excused himself and crawled into bed.

They were awakened in the middle of the night by repeated pounding on the door of the apartment. Roddy heard Ling pad across the living room in her flip-flops and then some conversation in Chinese. The other voice was a woman's, and it became increasingly shrill until evidently Ling let the woman into her apartment. There was more talk, slightly more subdued. Roddy picked up a note of desperation in the woman's voice. Suddenly the door burst open and the woman came into his room. She came to the end of his bed and stared fixedly at him. She was young and attractive in spite of her obvious agitation. She addressed him in Chinese. He sat up in bed and gestured. "I'm sorry, I don't understand." Ling came in behind her and ushered her out of the room. There was more talk, the woman's voice rising once again in pitch and volume. Roddy put on his dressing gown and came into the living room. "Is there anything I can do?"

"Sit with her for a moment while I go into the kitchen."

The woman sat opposite Roddy and gave him a hostile look. She got up and went into the bathroom. Ling reappeared with some tea.

"Where is she?"

"In the bathroom. What's the matter?"

"She's looking for some man. She's convinced he's in this apartment."

"How peculiar. Did she say why she thinks he's here?"

"She's rather hysterical. And of course she's speaking Cantonese." Roddy knew that Ling, being the daughter of a diplomat sent to the U.S. in the early 1940s by Chiang Kai-shek, spoke Mandarin. "I can manage up to a point, but I may have missed something. She refuses to leave. I called the police when I was in the kitchen. You can go back to bed if you like."

"I'm awake now. I can offer moral support."

"I was hoping for a little immoral support."

"At least you've managed to hang onto your sense of humour."

They drank tea while waiting for the woman to re-emerge from the bathroom. Eventually Ling went to check on her and discovered she'd locked herself in. She spoke to her through the locked door, trying to persuade her to come out and drink some tea. This went on for fifteen minutes. Ling cajoled, pleaded, and, finally, commanded her to come out of the bathroom. Her efforts were to no avail.

Ling returned from the hall and sat down across from Roddy. They gossiped about friends in Toronto until the police arrived. The young officer was brisk and courteous. He walked up to the bathroom door and spoke to the woman. For a while she refused to answer, but then poured out a long tirade. The policeman came back and said he would need to call for reinforcements. They would need to break down the door and they must have a policewoman present in case the woman accused them of sexual assault. Ling offered him tea, which he refused but then accepted. They sat in silence and waited until two more policemen arrived with a young woman in uniform. They forced the lock and the young woman was dragged away protesting loudly. They could hear her high-pitched voice as she was dragged down the hall. They watched from the window as the police car pulled away.

"What will they do with her?"

"Take her to the station for questioning, I suppose. If she calms down, they'll probably release her. She seemed to think

I had seduced her boyfriend. Apparently he's a university student."

"She's obviously a bit deranged."

"Poor thing. I was quite proud of my Cantonese. I don't have much occasion to use it except when I'm ordering meals and shopping. It's not as rusty as I imagined. Are you going back to bed?"

Roddy said he didn't think so.

THE NEXT AFTERNOON LING led Roddy into a seminar room where about twenty students sat at a long table. He looked around as Ling introduced him and realized that the boy he had met at the sauna was sitting at the far end of the table. He was already nervous about addressing this unfamiliar audience, and this unlikely coincidence threw him off even more. He got off to a poor start, speaking too quietly at first and then, as he realized some of the students were leaning forward to hear him, too loudly. He had decided to take a rather personal approach, explaining how as a teenaged student he had become interested in medieval art. He painted a picture of life on the Canadian prairies in the 1940s when he was growing up.

The students were unresponsive. They sat impassively as he became more and more nervous and uneasy. He cut short the last part of his talk about his early experience of art museums in Europe and offered to answer questions. Only one was forthcoming from a student who asked a rather complicated question about Duccio. Roddy launched into a detailed response and gradually realized that no one apart from the questioner was following what he was saying. He then asked the students to tell him about their favourite works of art. Two or three made rather perfunctory answers, no doubt out of a feeling of obligation to appear polite. Then Ling declared that their time was up. She thanked Roddy for sharing his insights and the students dispersed.

Roddy excused himself and went down the hall to the washroom. After a moment the boy from the sauna came in and stood at the next urinal. "I cannot go to sauna tomorrow," he said. "Can I come to apartment?"

Roddy hesitated. "All right, yes. If my friend is there you will be discreet, I trust."

The boy smiled at him and was gone. Roddy rejoined Ling, who took him downstairs to the senior common room. They both had a glass of whisky, which Roddy felt he richly deserved. "I'm afraid it didn't go over very well."

"Chinese students don't expect lecturers to talk about themselves. They don't understand why you would do such a thing. They are trained from an early age not to give away any information about themselves — in case it might be used against them."

"I wish you'd told me."

"I had no idea you'd take that tack. But no harm done."

"That boy at the end of the table, the one with the heavy eyebrows, who is he?"

"I have no idea. There were two or three students who are not part of my regular class. I suppose they were curious.

They must have heard that you might be a guest lecturer next year. I suppose you would like to go to a Chinese restaurant tonight for a change."

"That would be nice."

"I'll take you to one of the few places where they know how to cook some of the old imperial dishes. I can't bear coolie food."

The dinner involved tiny pancakes filled with seafood, grilled carcasses of tiny birds in a nest of crisp noodles, and a whole fish stuffed with a subtly flavoured combination of vegetables. Ling disdained to describe how these various dishes were prepared. She approved of the pancakes and the ortolans, but was disappointed in the fish. She promised to prepare a superior version for him when he returned from Beijing.

"I noticed Birgitta chatting you up last night out on the terrace. She phoned me at the office. She thinks she's convinced you to take up the university's offer."

"I am seriously considering it, although after my debacle this afternoon …"

"Don't worry. If you come, I'll see you get off on the right foot. You know I've really missed you out here. I think it's time we came to terms, you and I."

"Terms?"

"You must know I'm fond of you. You seem to enjoy my company. We're neither of us getting any younger."

Roddy gave her a sharp look.

"I know you're gay."

"I don't care for that word."

"You prefer to be called a 'perennial bachelor'? Come on, Roddy. This is the second half of the twentieth century."

"How long have you known about me?"

"Oh, for God's sake. Everybody knows about you. Your colleagues, your students. You can't seriously imagine you've been fooling anyone."

"My mother doesn't know."

"Your mother is ninety-two and deaf as a post. But I'd be willing to bet she does know."

"Are you really seriously proposing — what? A sort of *mariage blanc*?"

"You don't imagine I'd have gone to all the trouble of arranging for the university to invite you here if I weren't serious, do you?"

"But if everybody knows, as you say, wouldn't you feel embarrassed?"

"I'm not a blushing twenty-year-old in the 1950s. And I'm not naïve. I've had lovers, starting with old Professor Irving. Quite a few since then, actually. Shall I give you the details?"

"Good God, no. Let's not talk about it anymore." He looked away, then turned back to her. She was still looking at him intently. "I'll have to think about it, Ling."

Back in the apartment, Ling poured herself her usual nightcap. "Will you join me?"

"Perhaps this once."

She sat beside him and held his hand. It made him feel uneasy, but he felt it would be rude to withdraw from her small clutching fingers. He wondered whether she would propose further intimacy, but she finished her drink and retired to her bedroom. He sat for a considerable time looking out at the lights in the harbour and turning the day's events over in his mind. He could see that an arrangement with Ling might have real advantages, socially and from a career standpoint. Was it being dishonest to accept her offer for what he would have to admit were the wrong reasons? Perhaps not if he discussed it with her before committing himself. Could she accept that he would have liaisons on the side? He used to imagine settling down with another man, but so far he hadn't found one he wanted to live with. The ones he was attracted to were usually younger and rarely anything even close to his intellectual equals. As he grew older, the gap only widened. He climbed into bed but his mind kept circling around and around until just before dawn, when he finally dozed off.

LING ROSE EARLY AND left a note: she had a luncheon engagement and then a faculty meeting. She would be back by four-thirty. Birgitta had invited them for dinner. Roddy arose just before noon feeling groggy and a bit hungover. The note was reassuring. He would have his lover all to himself for two hours. He drank two cups of coffee and then went out for a brisk walk. He returned to the apartment and read *The Economist* as he waited for the bell to ring. Two o'clock came and then two-thirty. He was in a nervous state when the doorbell rang at a quarter to three. He sprang up and opened the door, and the boy stepped into the apartment. He looked around uneasily. Roddy gave him a kiss. "You know, I don't even know your name."

"You call me Peter."

The boy walked to the window and looked out. Roddy followed him and put a hand on his shoulder. The boy turned. Roddy smiled. "Do sit down. Can I make you some tea?"

"No, thank you." The boy sat on the sofa, a serious expression on his face.

Roddy sat beside him. He took the boy's hand and realized how much more excited he felt than when he had held Ling's hand the night before. *This is what I really want*, he thought. *I mustn't kid myself.*

"I only stay two minute."

"Why? I've been looking forward —"

The door opened. It was Ling. "The faculty meeting was cancelled," she called.

The boy quickly withdrew his hand from Roddy's grasp and stood up. Roddy stood as well. "This is Peter. He came to my lecture yesterday."

"I must apologize. A young woman came here. She come to find me. She is my fiancée. She follow me. I am sorry for her. Now I say goodbye."

"No, wait." Roddy placed a restraining hand on the boy's arm. "Peter, please — don't go."

But Peter was already heading to the door. He stopped and held out his hand to Roddy. "Goodbye." He opened the door and left.

"I don't understand what …"

"I think it's clear enough. You brought him here to have sex." Ling looked at Roddy levelly. "I'll make some tea. Or maybe we should have a drink."

"Not for me. I think I'll go for a walk."

"We're expected at Birgitta's at seven."

"I hope it's going to be an early night. You know I'm flying to Beijing at seven tomorrow morning."

"Right."

Roddy left immediately. Ling downed a healthy slug of whisky. She sat and assessed the situation. She was nothing if not a realist. Fond as she was of Roddy, and as passionate as she had been when she was with some of her former lovers, she had never let these relationships stand in the way of her career. She supposed that was why, one after another, they had all moved away from her. Somehow she had thought it might be different with Roddy. An intimacy built on a friendship between equals. Was it too late even for that? She didn't see why it had to be. And, yet, if this afternoon's incident was a harbinger of what could be expected, was she prepared for it? She poured another shot of whisky.

RODDY FOUND THE DINNER party a test of his endurance. Ling was drunk before they got there. She attacked several of the guests, particularly an American graduate student who had pronounced on the stultifying effect of the Communist regime on contemporary Chinese painting. At one point, she abandoned any semblance of scholarly argument and shouted,

"Oh, for God's sake, you pompous ignoramus, shut up." Roddy was concerned that she might become violent, but shortly after this outburst she fell off her chair. Although Ling protested, Roddy drove them home. Safely arrived in the garage of her apartment building, he took Ling by the elbow and propelled her along the hall into the elevator. He could not stop her from pouring out a tumbler of whisky, some of which she spilled on her shantung suit. She sat heavily on the sofa and glared at him.

"I've thought about it and decided you're right. You're too set in your ways to change now. And if you came here you might easily become an embarrassment. To yourself as well as to me. So that's that. I'm not getting up in the morning to see you off. You can call a cab. You're welcome to stay here when you come back from Beijing. I won't be here. I'm taking a group of students to Tokyo." She turned and looked out the window.

"I'm sorry, Ling." No answer. "I'm sure you're right."

"Of course I'm right. Not that it makes me feel any better."

LENORE

When Lenore Loring bit her housekeeper for the second time, her nieces decided it was necessary to move her into a home. As there was money to cover the costs, they decided that Buchanan Arms offered the best value. They stripped her of her diamond rings, which they put in a safety deposit box, thinned out her wardrobe, giving a few ancient ball gowns to the museum and much of the rest to Goodwill, and gave her housekeeper a handsome settlement.

The nieces were delighted to find that two of Lenore's oldest friends were living at the Buchanan Arms, but Lenore showed no interest in them until one of the women, Lily Montrose, suggested they get together for a game of bridge. Although Lenore seemed not to remember Lily she remembered most of the Goren Convention, and to Lily's delight they trounced their opponents, winning two straight rubbers. A few days later one of Lily's grandsons came to visit, and she made a special point of taking him up to meet Lenore. Lenore found the child poisonous and told Lily so. There were no more bridge games. She also told her nieces she had no interest in seeing them and they discontinued their monthly visits.

The priest from St. Alban's, which Lenore had attended sporadically for over thirty years, came to see her shortly after she moved into the Buchanan Arms. He quickly realized she had no intention of joining him in prayer. She told him how as a young girl she had wanted to be a missionary. His parents had been missionaries in China, so he talked to her about his boyhood memories. She listened with some interest before saying, "You're making this up to get on my good side. But I'm not leaving a single penny to the church."

The nurses at the Buchanan Arms were wary of Lenore, but they allowed her to keep a bottle of whisky in her room. She drank two shots in the morning, two in the afternoon, and two more after dinner. She frequently awoke in the middle of the night and had one more drink, then slept till after nine. As breakfast was at seven, she rarely ate it. She had never been much of a reader, although as a girl she had read *Black Beauty* and *David Copperfield* and *The Mill on the Floss*. Now she watched daytime soap operas. The nurses sometimes tried to talk with her about these shows, but although she had a few favourite characters, mainly crusty older women, she couldn't follow the plotlines and missed most of the dialogue.

She was watching one of these soaps, her first whisky of the afternoon in hand, when there was a knock on her door and a nurse announced briskly that there was a visitor to see her. She ushered in a young man in his late thirties, who smiled at her. She was annoyed at being interrupted in the middle of the program, though she didn't really understand what was going on, and said rather crossly, "Who are you?"

"Olivier Loring," came the reply. "Your grandson."

She eyed him sharply. "Nonsense."

"It is true we have not met. My father was your son, Mickey."

"Mickey?"

"Surely you remember?"

"Do I?" Then abruptly: "I always wanted a grandson." But it was Julian's son she had hoped for.

"My mother was Madeleine. She came here to visit you with my father."

"Little French tramp," she muttered, almost to herself. "What are you doing here? You're not going to get any of my money."

He gave her a smile. "I was curious. I have heard a lot about you."

Lenore snorted, but his smile intrigued her. There was something very familiar about it, though she couldn't quite place it.

"My mother sometimes spoke of you. She thought you did not like her."

"She was French. You speak French?"

"I have lived most of my life in France. And in Italy."

"Venice. The canals were full of garbage and dead cats. Would you like some whisky?"

"Would you?"

"There's a bottle on the dresser."

He took her glass and refilled it. "Water?" His smile seemed to echo something, something from the past.

He handed her glass back to her. She took a healthy gulp, dribbling on her dressing gown. She eyed him sharply. "You look like a Loring. Why are you here?"

"It's natural to want to meet one's grandmother."

"Not much about my family is natural, if you ask me. They never come to see me."

"I'm sorry."

"I don't like them. They don't like me." She suddenly grinned at him. "You're better looking than any of them."

"Thank you."

"Handsome is as handsome does. You'd better go now."

"Can I come and see you again?"

"What for?"

"Just because I'd like to," he hesitated, "Granny." He came toward her and tried to plant a kiss on her cheek. She turned her head away from him. As he went out the door she called out, "All right." She took a sip of whisky and turned back to the television.

Julian was her firstborn, and from the moment she saw him she adored him. It was clear he was bright: he used big words at an early age. He was also allergic and cranky. Lenore had been a nurse and she treated him as her little patient, making special meals for him and putting up with his frequent temper tantrums. He basked in her attention, but when he reached his mid-teens he tired of her possessiveness. He began to have girlfriends and at twenty he married Cissy, who was already pregnant with their first child. Julian quit school and went to work for his father. Then Cissy had a miscarriage. Lenore might have been expected to be sympathetic, but instead it confirmed her poor opinion of Cissy. The girl was depressed and Julian didn't know how to deal with her. At Lenore's suggestion they moved into the Loring house. Lenore wanted Julian close to her and took every opportunity to undermine Cissy.

A few months later, there was a knock on the door around eleven o'clock at night and a familiar voice. "Anybody home?"

"Mickey ..." Julian jumped up from the foot of Lenore's bed. "What the hell?"

Lenore was not easily taken off her guard, but she found herself almost paralyzed as she looked at her younger son standing in the doorway, his deeply tanned face split by a mischievous grin. She had not experienced the same deep feelings for Mickey that she had for Julian. She had desperately wanted a son and when Julian was born she was satisfied. Mickey was an afterthought, as they used to say. Having come from a big family herself, she had no sentimental craving for a large brood; she knew too well how little attention and encouragement there was to go around.

Julian gave his brother a hug. They had been close as boys, competitive and yet bonded by their ongoing skirmish with their parents. Julian had knuckled under and gone to work for his father, but Mickey had escaped, winning a Rhodes Scholarship and then persuading his father to finance him through two further years at the École Pol in Paris. Mickey was a good athlete, something his father envied. Mickey was what his father would have liked to have been and Jarvis indulged him, while trying to pretend to himself he treated both boys equally.

Mickey looked back into the hall. "Don't be shy," he said. "Come in." He ushered in a slender girl with long dark hair, whose tan was, if possible, of a deeper hue than Mickey's. "My family. My mother, and this is brother Julian and his wife Cissy."

Madeleine smiled at Julian and held up her cheeks to be kissed. This European custom had not yet caught on in Toronto and Lenore considered it downright brazen, but she held her tongue. Madeleine moved towards her, holding out her hand. With some hesitation Lenore took it, and noticed a light brown down on the girl's arms, even a tiny tuft of hair in her armpits poking through the cap sleeves of her flowered summer dress.

Cissy stood up and walked over to Madeleine. "I love your dress. It's so simple."

"It's Christian Dior. It was terribly expensive. My father bought it for me."

Mickey and Madeleine stayed for two weeks. Lenore was sure Madeleine was making a play for Julian. One night she was certain she heard them kissing as she stood outside Julian's room. She thought about bursting in on them. She was sure she could hear them kissing. Silently she made her way back down the hall to her own room.

A WEEK AFTER OLIVIER'S first visit, he returned to find Lenore lying back on the pillows of her bed, asleep, her mouth open with a thin dribble of saliva running down her chin. She opened her eyes to see him sitting in her armchair with a sheaf of yellow tulips in his hand.

"How did you get in here?"

"They said I could come up on my own." He advanced towards her and held out the flowers.

She stared at them balefully. "I hate yellow," she said, and buzzed for the nurse.

"I'm going on a trip. To Mexico."

"You'll get diarrhea. If you're not shot first."

The nurse looked in at the door. "Bring us some tea," Lenore commanded. The nurse scuttled away.

"I wanted to say goodbye."

"We have nothing in common."

"Except blood."

"They say blood is thicker than water. It's not true."

He shrugged. "I have no close relatives. Except you."

"You have cousins, but I wouldn't sic any of them onto you. Will you come back on your way home?"

"I don't know. I don't really have a home."

The nurse arrived with the tea tray. "Shall I pour it?"

"He'll do that."

Olivier poured two cups and handed one to Lenore.

"I always have tea in the afternoon. My parents drank tea and nothing else. They were teetotallers. I signed the pledge when I was fourteen." She gave a delighted cackle. "Just pour an ounce into the cup," she said, indicating the bottle on the dresser. "Mickey used to talk about going to live in Mexico. He spoke the lingo. Do you?"

"A bit. I'm not really fluent." He smiled. That smile again. She knew it would come to her if she really thought about it.

"You'll make your way with that smile. I suppose you thought I hadn't noticed. You turn it on like a tap."

"Do I?"

"I'm not as dumb as some people think."

"People?"

There was a pause.

"You don't have much to say for yourself. Mickey was a talker. Never shut up. Julian liked to talk too. It was about all they had in common."

She closed her eyes, calling up their faces from memory. And then she knew.

"Julian was a worker. Mickey never did anything much. Went to school till he was nearly thirty. Then he died. What do you do?"

"I make films. Documentaries for television."

"Are they shown here?"

"Not usually. I could bring you a DVD."

"I wouldn't understand it anyway. You better go now."

He walked up to her. This time she didn't turn away, but let him brush her wrinkled cheek with his lips.

"Send me a postcard."

He left and she stared balefully at the yellow flowers. She remembered going to visit her mother after her first miscarriage.

HATTIE MCCASLIN SAT IN a rocking chair in the kitchen, darning socks. The room was just as Lenore had remembered it: the table covered with checkered oilcloth, and on it two pressed glass bowls, one for sugar and one for teaspoons; the big cast-iron stove at the back of which a teapot sat warming, the tea getting ever blacker; the painted yellow floor she had scrubbed so many times as a girl that she had come to loathe the colour.

Hattie didn't get up, but grimaced at her daughter. "I'm sorry for your trouble. I guess you wasn't meant to have any with them slim hips." Hattie's own shape was ample, not surprising after bearing nine children, though even in her wedding picture she was hardly slender. Hattie had often made fun of Lenore. "Skinnikins" she'd called her. "You should put some flesh on your bones," she'd say. "A man likes something he can hold onto."

"What's the good of being married if I can't have kids?" Lenore lamented.

"Well now, Lenore, you'll have them if you're meant to and if you ain't, you must grin and bear it. At least you've got a man what's a good provider. Count your blessings."

"I want to be more than just a housekeeper. I've always wanted to help people. I wanted to be a missionary in China."

"That wasn't meant to be."

"I'd like to go back to nursing, but Jarvis won't let me."

"Likely he knows best. You was never cut out to be a real hard worker. Oh, you're willin' enough, I'll give you that. None of the others could peel potatoes as fast as you."

Lenore looked at the yellow floor, but said nothing.

"You'd better have some tea. There's some made up on the back of the stove. It's nice and strong. You could trot a mouse on it."

Lenore didn't want her mother's tea, but she also didn't want to offend her. She poured two cups, putting four spoonfuls of sugar in one and handing it to Hattie, who stirred it, poured it into the saucer, and slurped it up.

"I was thinking I might come and stay here with you. Help out."

"We're managin' just fine."

"You're not getting any younger."

"I wouldn't feel right you bein' here, Lenore, I might as well tell you plain. Your job is to look after your husband. He treats you good, don't he?"

Lenore didn't answer. She dug in her purse, pulled out an envelope, and gave it to her mother.

"What's this for?" Hattie opened the envelope and pulled out five ten-dollar bills.

"I saved it from my housekeeping money. I want you to buy yourself something nice."

"You're a good girl, Lenore. Even if you do have some odd notions. And maybe you'll have a kiddie after all."

Lenore was just able to hold her breath long enough to cross the room and get out the door. She sat on the porch swing and had a really good cry.

LENORE WAS LYING ON the floor the next time Olivier came to see her. She had tried to pull herself up but had only succeeded in knocking over the little table beside her bed, spilling its contents on the floor: a small framed photograph of Julian as a boy, a box of Kleenex, and a milk-glass hen, in which she kept her hairpins, that had come from the family farmhouse.

Olivier lifted her under the arms and set her down on the bed. "Granny, what happened?"

"I fell out of bed. You're not to tell the nurse or they'll tie me up. Promise."

"Sure you haven't broken something?"

"What if I have?"

"Take my arm and we'll walk across the room."

She glared at him but did as she was told.

"Does it hurt anywhere?"

"No," she lied. Her left hip was sore, but she was determined to ignore it. "I want to sit in the chair." He steered her back to the armchair and eased her into it, looking down on her to make sure she was all right. "Don't stand over me like that. Go and sit on the bed."

He looked across at her and she looked back with something almost like a grin, pleased with herself for not having been caught lying on the floor by one of the nurses. He smiled back. Was it possible? This time she was sure of it.

"How was your trip to ... where was it?"

"Mexico."

"With your girlfriend. See, I don't forget everything."

"She wasn't exactly a girlfriend."

"Gave you the lemon, eh?"

"She had some interesting friends. She introduced me to a Mexican filmmaker. We're going to work together on a film."

"You'll need money."

"Yes."

"How much?"

"Maybe fifty thousand to get started."

"What would you say if I gave it to you?"

"Why would you?"

"Because I feel like it. My chequebook is in the top right-hand drawer of my dresser. Under my stockings. Go and get it."

Olivier stood up. He looked at her.

"And my pen. Quickly, before I change my mind."

He did as he was told. She took the pen and began to write. "How do you spell your name?'"

"Loring?"

"Your French name."

He spelled out "Olivier" for her.

Panting slightly from the effort, she finished writing the cheque, tore it out, and handed it to him.

He looked at it incredulously. "Thank you. Are you sure you can afford this?"

"That's my business. If you say anything to the nurse about finding me on the floor I'll call the bank and tell them to cancel it. Now come here and give me a kiss."

He planted a light kiss on her cheek.

"On the mouth." She clutched his arm. Her lips were trembling. "Now go."

He stopped in the doorway and turned towards her, smiling. Julian's smile. He must be Julian's child. She was sure of it.

WILL YOU JOIN THE DANCE?

Just before Carson graduated from Upper Canada College his father, Edgar, took him to lunch at the Toronto Club. He ordered veal and ham pie, a Waldorf salad, and a bottle of Chablis. Edgar complimented his son on his final marks — six firsts, and seconds in all his other papers except trigonometry. Edgar asked what university the boy was hoping to attend and Carson responded he supposed either McGill or Toronto or maybe King's in Halifax. Edgar thought that a small college like Mount Allison offered a more intimate and personal experience. He expected that Carson would once again be a counsellor at Ahmek, the boys' camp he had attended as a teenager. When Carson said that he was planning to spend his summer with a modern dance company, Edgar was taken aback. He was unaware that Carson had been taking dance classes on Saturday mornings for some time. Edgar and his wife Verity were generous supporters of the arts — Verity was on the boards of the Art Gallery and the Symphony. But Carson had never shown much interest in anything aesthetic. He had been a reasonably good athlete at school, winning awards in track and field. Perhaps this would be an advantage to him as a dancer. Edgar had heard that dancers had a reputation for being promiscuous and probably homosexual; when he discussed Carson's plan with his wife, he kept these suspicions to himself. Verity suggested that dance was probably a phase the boy was going through; in any case, she felt they should encourage him in this new interest. Edgar shrugged and agreed not to interfere.

EDGAR AND VERITY WENT to the first performance in which Carson was to dance. He appeared in the last piece on the program, a new work by the company's founder and principal choreographer, Jeremy Humbert. To the recorded music of a Bach toccata, eight dancers in brief, flesh-coloured costumes stretched and writhed in angular, abstract movements meant to convey the concept or meaning of a reaching for something higher. There was nothing sensual about the piece, but rather a sort of energized spirituality. Verity found herself unexpectedly moved by the performance. Edgar was less enthusiastic. They remained in their seats after the piece finished, until Carson appeared in jeans and a sweatshirt accompanied by an older man — bald, bearded, but still quite muscular.

"This is our choreographer, Jeremy Humbert."

"Good of you to come, Mr. and Mrs. Warren. Your son shows real promise."

Verity gave Jeremy her most charming smile. She was pleased and displeased at the same time. She did not want to believe that Carson was going to pursue a career as a dancer and she knew Edgar would be even less enthused. He was counting on Carson to take a law degree and then come into his firm.

"We're going to a little restaurant down the street to get something to eat. Why don't you join us?" Jeremy asked.

Verity explained that she had another engagement she must go on to, but Edgar agreed to go with the dancers. He found himself seated between Carson and Jeremy at The Golden Apple. He ordered a Caesar. The dancers talked amongst themselves about things such as not quite managing the second lift or the final spin. Jeremy asked Edgar if he had ever seen the company before; Edgar had to admit he had not. Verity had planned to attend when she was on the board of the National Ballet, but she was on the board of the Symphony at the time as well, and he had been fundraising for the university; they could only do so many things at once. Fortunately the university had achieved its target and the Symphony was almost back in the black.

"Would you consider being a member of our board?"

"I'd have to think about it."

He discussed the idea with Verity when he got home. He drank a glass of Scotch in their living room under a number of modern paintings he would have considered obscene had they not been sold to him as art. Verity encouraged him to accept. This was a small company and being a board member would probably not be all that time-consuming. They could undoubtedly use a lawyer on their board and he could keep an eye on Carson.

EDGAR BROUGHT TO THE board a certain skill in resolving disputes and this was soon appreciated by the other members, mostly middle-aged women who were more interested in the food served at their meetings than the art of the dance. Edgar gave them a bang-up lunch for their annual meeting at the York Club and found himself elected vice president.

UNLIKE MOST OF THE other members, he went to rehearsals when invited. Somewhat to his surprise he found that he enjoyed watching the process as it evolved. He enjoyed hearing Jeremy's stories about working with Martha Graham in the early sixties. "The old witch was so jealous of our young bodies that she used to beat us with her arthritic hands." The dancers were putting together a new work choreographed by Ryan Berg, Jeremy's protégé and, Edgar learned from his board colleagues, his sometime lover. The dancers responded quickly and enthusiastically to Ryan's suggestions. They seemed a very compatible group, eager to offer suggestions and try new moves. During their breaks they indulged in a bit of friendly horseplay, pretending to be a matador confronting a bull or a cowboy galloping over the plains. It was clear Carson was having a good time and that the others readily accepted him as one of them.

Edgar could not detect any overt romantic alliances within

the company. Carson seemed to be able to handle close physical contact with both men and women. Edgar knew that his son had yet to have a sustained relationship with a woman; he went to parties and dances with various girls, but none of them seemed to be more than good friends. Edgar told himself that his son was only nineteen — perhaps he was a late bloomer.

At the next concert Edgar sat in the front row in his Savile Row suit, fingering his watch chain. He applauded enthusiastically as the younger members of the audience whooped and hollered. He was particularly taken with Valerie, a young dancer who performed a flamenco-inspired solo of her own devising; he actually shouted *"Brava!"* when she finished. He was introduced to her at the reception afterwards and offered to take her to lunch at his club. She responded that she never ate during the day. He then suggested dinner, an offer she accepted with a flirtatious smile.

Ryan joined them and complimented Valerie on her performance. He spoke of an idea he had for a much larger work, which would require some funding outside their regular budget. Edgar suggested that they have a gala fundraiser at which they would have a contest of various dance forms: the tango, the waltz, the Charleston. Ryan considered this a brilliant idea and Edgar promised to invite some of his friends and their wives.

Edgar had been more or less faithful to his wife throughout their twenty-nine years of marriage, but he was aware that many of his wealthy contemporaries had mistresses and that the strict Presbyterian morality he had grown up with had in recent times been considerably eroded. He remembered a New Year's Eve party he had attended two years before, at which the hostess had entertained her former husband with his third wife, a bank president had arrived with his wife and her boyfriend, and the hostess's current lover's ex-wife had arrived with her new girlfriend. He had briefly wondered if he was missing out on something.

For his dinner date with Valerie he chose an out-of-the-way restaurant. He introduced her to oysters on the half-shell, Chablis, and lobster ravioli. She was duly appreciative, but not very talkative. She laughed at his jokes and seemed interested in his stories about his recent travels to Bayreuth to see a new production of Wagner's *Ring*. He had seen some eighteen productions of the cycle and confessed to being a bit of a Ring nut.

After dinner Valerie invited him back to her apartment for a nightcap. She lived in the basement of a house in Cabbagetown. There was a chair, a bed, a table, and some Indian hangings on the walls. He sat in the chair while she poured him a glass of Cointreau. She put on a record of Arvo Pärt, lit a stick of incense, and then curled up on the frayed kilim at his feet. She asked him about his work and he told her that he bought and sold companies, which involved frequent travel to London, Paris, Madrid, Milan, Buenos Aires, and Hong Kong. She confessed she had never been anywhere and would love to go to some of these exotic places. Edgar smiled. "We shall see," he said. "But

I hate to see you in this dump. You don't even have cooking facilities."

"I'm used to it," she answered. "Anyway, dancers don't eat much."

"You tucked right in tonight at dinner."

"That will last me three days."

There was a silence during which Edgar was aware of her supple back leaning against his legs. She turned towards him, brushing his knee with her hand. He stood up. "I must be going. I'm in the office every morning at nine. But I think we'll have to find you some better living quarters."

She stood close to him and brushed his mouth with her lips. "Thank you — for everything."

He hesitated a moment, smiled and headed for the door.

DRIVING HOME IN HIS Jaguar, he replayed the events of the evening in his mind. The girl was available, that was clear. But he would take his time. He went upstairs, put on his silk pyjamas, and crawled into bed beside Verity. She was already asleep. It had been some time since they had had sex. Could he still function? They had pills to deal with that problem. He thought of Valerie in her slinky silk dress with its low-cut neckline revealing her limited cleavage. He turned on his side, away from Verity, and soon drifted off.

The gala was a huge success. Thirty-two of Verity and Edgar's friends attended at one-hundred-and-fifty dollars apiece. The silent auction netted an additional three-hundred-and-sixty dollars. Valerie lured Edgar onto the floor to demonstrate his Charleston, and although they didn't win they were loudly applauded. Carson and a Japanese dancer won the tango contest. Jeremy and Verity performed a sedate waltz. Edgar managed to have a few minutes alone with Valerie when she went outside for a cigarette. He told her he had found a condo he could rent for her. It was only a few blocks from the dance studio. He worried she might not be willing to accept his offer, but she thanked him demurely and agreed to move in at the end of the month. He offered to drive her home, but she said she had other plans. He was somewhat relieved. He didn't want Verity to see that he was taking a special interest in any of the young dancers.

EDGAR TREATED RYAN TO lunch a week later and handed him a cheque for ten thousand dollars towards the cost of his new piece. Ryan accepted with gratitude, but pointed out that this generous donation might not sit very well with Jeremy, he being the artistic director. Edgar said not to worry; he would clear the donation with Jeremy. Edgar made his donation on condition that the new work should contain a major solo for Valerie. Ryan had expected Edgar would want the work to showcase the talents of his son. Edgar smiled, but did not comment. He hoped Verity's observation that dance was just a passing phase for Carson was right; although, if the kid was enjoying himself, it seemed harmless enough.

A few days later, Edgar's secretary announced there was a Mr. Cardozza to see him. Edgar had never heard of him, but when his secretary told him his visitor was connected with "some dance company," Edgar decided to have him shown in. Cardozza was a rather scruffy-looking man in his late fifties with several days' growth of beard, scuffed cowboy boots, and a jean jacket. He sat rather uneasily across the desk from Edgar, coughing nervously. "Mind if I smoke?"

"I'm afraid you can't smoke here. What can I do for you?"

"I come to talk to you about Jeremy. Me and him was lovers." There was a pause. "I figure I gotta warn you." Edgar looked at him steadily. "I was a pretty good dancer. He brung me up here from New York. I was the hottest thing in the company. He set a lot of his best pieces on me. But a lot of them were based on my ideas which he stole from me. I didn't mind 'cause I was the star. But then a younger dancer come along and Jeremy lost interest in me. He took up with this other guy and then dropped me from the company like a hot potato. See, the thing is, he likes young skin. Guess you know he makes all his men dancers audition in the nude." Cardozza leaned back and looked at Edgar with a malicious grin.

Edgar was determined to preserve his composure. He paused for a moment and looked at his visitor. "Do you have a job?"

"Yeah. I'm a caretaker, you might say."

"Your story is interesting, but why should I believe you? Jeremy Humbert is a highly respected artist."

"Like I said. I figured I should warn you, before you got in too deep."

"Do you need money?"

"I wouldn't refuse a contribution."

Edgar got out his chequebook and wrote a cheque for five hundred dollars. His visitor grinned and pocketed it. "Thanks. I can tell you're a real gentleman."

Edgar rang for his secretary who promptly appeared. "Show Mr. Carpaccio out."

"Cardozza. Take it easy, okay?" He held out his hand, but Edgar declined to shake it. He sat and pondered this new information. Later at home he questioned Carson about the nude auditions.

"Oh, yeah, Jeremy's gay as a goose. He gets the guys to take off their clothes whenever he can. He loves to watch us in the shower. But he's harmless. He only pursues the ones who are interested."

"It doesn't bother you?"

"Nah. There were some gays at school. So what? Live and let live."

At dinner that night Edgar wondered if he should tell Verity about his visitor. But before he could say anything Verity spoke up. "I hear you've given Ryan some money towards a new piece."

"Yes. What he told me about it sounded very interesting."

"Shouldn't you have approached Jeremy first? He *is* the artistic director."

Edgar pondered Verity's words. She was more experienced as a board member of artistic institutions than he. But he had begun to worry about Jeremy. As Ryan had told him, the strain of running the company and the administration was having a negative effect on Jeremy's creativity. Ryan had suggested that Jeremy should perhaps consider stepping down as artistic director. He could stay on as resident choreographer and concentrate on his own work.

Valerie invited Edgar to dinner in her new flat. She prepared a vegetarian frittata with mushrooms. She wore a tight-fitting dress, which she confessed was one of her costumes. Flitting about the apartment in bare feet, she lit candles and put on a CD of Debussy piano music. Edgar watched her with delight and a growing sense of excitement. He was sure she would invite him into her bed before the evening was out.

When she did, their lovemaking was slow and easy; he was gratified when she rewarded his efforts with little squeals of pleasure. When he left her, he drove home in a daze. He could still make love to a woman. He couldn't wait for their next encounter.

Edgar began seeing Valerie twice a week. They didn't always have sex; sometimes she would improvise a dance for him or just sit beside him on the sofa, holding his hand and cuddling up to him. Occasionally he would take her to dinner, always to a different restaurant. He took pleasure in introducing her to French and Italian cuisine. She reciprocated by getting him to try Vietnamese and Thai eateries. Sometimes, he would drop by on his way home from the office. He had retained a key and liked to surprise her. She bought a bottle of single malt whisky to pour him pre-coital libations.

Edgar decided that he would shepherd a proposal for Ryan to take over the position of artistic director from Jeremy through the board. He was met with very little resistance. The board voted and the arrangement was scheduled to take effect the first of August. It was decided to have a party to honour Jeremy — a gala evening with performances of two of Jeremy's signature works, plus tribute speeches by several former dancers in the company as well as Edgar, who had just been promoted to president of the board when his predecessor had to undergo heart surgery. Both Ryan and Jeremy responded to his speech. Jeremy concluded by saying that for the past thirty years he had been trying to make love to Toronto, but most nights Toronto had a headache. Edgar provided a catered buffet supper and several cases of Prosecco. Toasts were drunk and there was much chatter and laughter. Afterwards, the dancers went on to Jeremy's house where, already tipsy, they played a series of games: adult versions of tag and hide-and-seek, ending in something that Ryan told Edgar resembled nothing so much as a Roman orgy. Edgar regretted his decision not to attend.

A week later, Edgar arrived at Valerie's flat and let himself in with his key. There was the sound of music, which he recognized as Debussy's *La Mer*. He opened the bedroom door and was surprised to see two figures writhing under the Indian bedspread. He walked over and pulled the sheet off the bed, revealing Valerie fellating a young man. The young man was Carson.

Valerie raised her head.

All three were silent.

"Would you please go now?" she finally demanded.

Edgar withdrew.

He sat in his Jaguar, shaking. He was angry and shocked. He had considered the idea that Carson might indeed be gay. Obviously this was not the case. But it was Valerie's deception that pained him. He had not imagined that she was a virgin, but to have sex with his own son? He drove home and had a double whisky. He sat across from Verity and toyed with the lamb chops the maid had set before him.

"Are you not well, Edgar?"

"I'm a bit off my game."

He went into the library, sank into in his wing chair, and poured another double whisky. He waited to hear Carson come in. He put on a CD of the Lebewohl that Wotan sings to Brünnhilde at the end of *Die Walküre* and thought of Valerie. He realized he was being sentimental, but decided to indulge himself. He had yet to let his emotions rule his life. If he wanted to enjoy his moment of self-pity, surely he was entitled to it. He went up to his dressing room and lay down on the cot. The idea of climbing into bed next to Verity seemed grotesque. It did not take long for him to fall asleep.

FOR THE NEXT TWO weeks, Edgar went to the office as usual. He had lunches with friends and business associates at his club. He tried not to think of Valerie, but he couldn't banish her from his consciousness. By now he was not so much angry as wistful. He revelled in his feelings of lost illusions.

On the Tuesday of the third week, Valerie telephoned him. She wanted to see him again, if only for a drink. He hesitated, but agreed to come to her apartment that afternoon on his way home. She was wearing jeans and a T-shirt with *Nothing is Forever* printed across it. She poured him a drink and sat opposite him.

"I'm not going to apologize. You must have realized I'm a free spirit."

He couldn't resist putting the pin in. "I was hoping to take you to Paris."

"It wouldn't work. You wouldn't be able to keep up with me."

"Touché."

"I'd like to remain friends. You can still fuck me once in a while if you want. I am fond of you."

Edgar winced. "We live in different worlds." He finished off his whisky. "I should be going." He stood up. "I'll pay your rent here until the end of the year."

She kissed him lightly on the lips. "You are a nice man."

"I guess that's the problem."

JEREMY WAS BECOMING IMPOSSIBLE. Temper tantrums in class and in the office. Picking on students he had always been kind and nurturing towards. He had insisted that their major performance at Harbourfront should be made up entirely of his own works. Ryan came to Edgar. "Either I'm the artistic director of this company or I'm not," he said. Edgar decided to deal with the situation firmly. He informed Jeremy that he would have to leave.

"I'm the founder of the company. I have a huge reputation."

"Then you won't have difficulty finding work elsewhere."

Jeremy could see Edgar was implacable. "I suppose you realize it's generally believed in the company that Ryan set you up with Valerie."

Edgar was infuriated; he couldn't bring himself to wish Jeremy good luck. He drove home at top speed. That night, at dinner, he told Verity about dismissing Jeremy. She shrugged it off as one of the things a board president had to deal with. "You've enjoyed your time with the dance company on the whole, haven't you? Flirting with all those pretty young women?"

Did she know about Valerie? There were one or two women on the board that were good friends of Verity's. It would be typical of her to stay silent. He knew she enjoyed the life they had made together: the dinner parties, the receptions, the trips to Europe. She wouldn't give that life up lightly. Maybe he would continue to see Valerie.

Edgar had decided not to confront his son. What would be gained by that? Carson was still living at home, though he rarely ate dinner with his parents. Father and son avoided each other. Late in August Edgar invited Carson to lunch again at his club. Cold lobster with garlic mayonnaise and a bottle of Chablis. He waited until they had finished dessert.

"I've been thinking about our discussion as to where you should attend university," he said. "I'll be paying your fees of course. I've decided you'll have a much better experience at Mount Allison. So that's settled. Right?"

MONTREAL REVISITED

When Teddy Sutherland received an invitation from Piers Walton to his wedding in Montreal he was surprised. It would be Piers's second marriage, but whether his first wife had died or they had divorced Teddy didn't know. He hadn't seen Piers for more than twenty-five years. Back in the late fifties, when he was an undergraduate, Teddy sometimes travelled to Montreal for fraternity weekends. He had a crush on Piers who was one of the McGill brothers. He knew it wasn't reciprocated, but Piers and he enjoyed each other's company. Piers was a bit of a clown, as well as what in the parlance of the day was known as an "ass man." On one occasion the two had shared a French-Canadian girl, Teddy's first three-way. The next morning they went to mass. Piers was Catholic and Teddy, although he wasn't religious, enjoyed the ritual: the incense, the chanting. He would have liked to take communion, but Piers said this was forbidden unless he converted.

Upon graduation, Teddy accepted a job with a Montreal brokerage house. When, three months later, he discovered he had passed the government exams for the Department of Trade and Commerce, he moved to Ottawa. He was offered a marginally higher salary, but the main reason he moved was that the government job was much more prestigious. He went to Montreal almost every weekend, not only to escape Ottawa but to get to know another aspect of the city, hanging out in the bars of rue St-Laurent where he consorted with a variety of low-life characters: *fifis*, transvestites, and a few older queens, some of them distinguished critics or animators working at the National Film Board. They introduced him to The Gay Apollo on rue Guy, where he watched male strippers, young guys from the Laurentides or the Gaspé who were prepared to bare their bodies for money. They occasionally suggested coming back to his hotel room for a night of uninhibited sex, which he declined out of a sense of caution more than a lack of interest. At the time, there was nothing like this on offer in Toronto or Ottawa.

In 1959 Teddy married Melanie, a girl he had been dating in Ottawa, the daughter of a cabinet minister. He didn't tell her of his attraction to men, knowing that this would have put paid to their courtship. His career demanded that he marry a suitable young woman; he was attracted to Melanie and they were accounted a handsome couple. She was, if not conventionally pretty, vivacious and accommodating, and took easily to the life of a rising young civil servant. They bought a house in New Edinburgh before it became fashionable and gave parties that attracted some of the brightest young people in the civil service as well as young parliamentarians and a few artists. Teddy and Melanie had an active sex life; he looked back on his homosexual adventures as a phase he had outgrown. It was not as though he'd done anything much, he told himself; he'd just liked to look. A few years later, he realized he was lucky to have "crossed over" before the Department, under pressure from the Americans, began clearing out the considerable number of closet queers in their ranks. If the RCMP had anything about his early activities in his secret dossier, they must have decided to overlook it.

Teddy returned to Ottawa from his posting in Copenhagen. He and Melanie had been separated for a decade. Melanie, who had taken a graduate degree in anthropology, had been offered a job at the Museum of Civilization. They had remained on good terms and had dinner twice with longtime friends. They were good company, but after a week or so Teddy was bored. He decided to visit Montreal before he took up his new posting in Jakarta. He stayed at the Ritz. He invited Piers and his new wife, Thérèse, for dinner. Piers was now bald and wore rimless glasses. Thérèse was a knockout. They had drinks in the Maritime Bar, ate Brome Lake duckling, and drank two bottles of Vacqueyras. After dinner, they went to a bistro on rue Ste-Catherine which Piers had heard about but never visited. Thérèse had told him there was a good young jazz trio playing there. It was a tacky bar, festooned with Christmas tree lights and Mylar strips agitated by an electric fan. The clientele was sparse: a few older gay men in leather or cowboy gear, a few kids garbed in black — which was apparently *de rigueur* among the student population. The MC was a drag queen whose patter was spiked with bitchy remarks about audience members. Initially Piers and Thérèse were amused, but after the first set they decamped. Teddy sat alone with a whisky and soda for one set, then decided he needed to get some fresh air. He wandered along rue Ste-Catherine and stopped in front of a gay strip bar. I'll just have one drink for auld lang syne, he thought. He sat at the bar and watched as a young man swung around a metal pole in a pair of pink briefs before shedding them and starting to masturbate.

"Some big cock," said the man beside him, a guy in his early forties with a lean face and a greying brush cut. He had grey-green eyes and a crooked grin. Teddy thought there was something familiar about him. The guy returned his look and suddenly laughed. "You don't remember me, hein?"

"I'm not sure ..."

"Teddy, right? We met at The Gay Apollo maybe twenty-five years ago. I used to dance there. You were a regular on weekends. I wore a gold lamé jockstrap. Trashy, hein? Who would have thought I would end up as a successful interior decorator with my own shop on Bishop Street?"

"I'm sorry. I'm afraid I've forgotten your name."

"I used to call myself Sebastien. My real name is Sylvain."

The kid, having achieved an impressive erection, stood

up and hung his briefs on his upright cock. He bowed to the applause from the spectators and blew a kiss towards Teddy's companion.

"You come here often?"

"Sometimes. I like young skin. Can I buy you a drink?"

"I've had enough. More than enough, really. I'd better get back to my hotel."

Teddy stood up and started to weave towards the door. Sylvain caught up to him and took his arm. They stood teetering on the sidewalk. Sylvain held onto him and hailed a cab, then got in with him. When they reached the Ritz, he paid the cabby and steered Teddy through the lobby into the elevator. Teddy found his key. Sylvain opened the door of his bedroom and propelled him over to the bed. He took off Teddy's shoes before Teddy collapsed on the bed with a bleary "Good night."

The next morning when Teddy woke up, his mouth felt like "a motorman's mitt" as Piers used to say. Being a steady drinker, he had never really suffered from a severe hangover before. He realized he was still wearing his shirt and socks but that his trousers and underpants had been removed. Next to him in the double bed was Sylvain, who turned his head and looked at him with his grey-green pussycat eyes. He took Teddy's hand and placed it on his hard cock. They kissed and cuddled for a few minutes and then moved on. After both of them had come, Sylvain asked about breakfast.

"Room service?"

"Let's go down to the dining room. I like my Eggs Benedict hot."

They showered together and dressed. Downstairs, the maître d' greeted Sylvain with a wink. "*Bonjour*, M. Lemieux." He showed them to a table in a secluded nook. "*Vous voulez la même comme d'habitude?*"

Sylvain nodded.

"*Et pour votre ami?*"

"*Même chose?*"

Teddy nodded. There was a short silence. "I'm rather ashamed of myself."

"Why? You're not quite the cute numéro you were, but you are still a very sexy man."

"I'm also a married man with three grown children."

"I'm married too. To my business partner. Six years we are together."

"Congratulations. She won't wonder where you were last night?"

"I'll tell *him* I met an old friend. We don't exactly have an open marriage but we give each other permission to stray once in a while. And you? You have been completely faithful to your wife?"

"We've been separated for over ten years."

The Eggs Benedict arrived and were demolished fairly rapidly. "I must go. My shop opens at ten. Shall we meet again while you're in Montreal?"

"I'm only here for another day."

"As you wish. It was very pleasant to be with you again."

Sylvain stood up, leaned across the table, and kissed Teddy. Teddy looked around. Nobody seemed to be watching.

Because it was a fine spring day, Teddy decided to go for a walk along Sherbrooke Street. The street had not changed that much: a few new tall buildings but many of the turreted mansions built by distillers and railway barons remained, along with the church of St. Andrew and St. Paul and the Musée des Beaux-Arts. He passed the neo-classical gates of McGill and Royal Victoria College with its statue of the Queen-Empress in bronze. He thought that Montreal was like a woman who was still attractive, although a bit past her prime.

On an impulse Teddy decided to climb Mount Royal. He remembered the first time he had visited Montreal, when he was nine and had stayed with his uncle; they had driven to the top and looked out over the city with its domes and spires. There were no tall buildings back then. His uncle had shown him the sights of the town: the basilica of Notre-Dame with its richly painted ceiling; Dominion Square surrounded by Edwardian office buildings; the elegant Windsor Hotel, where they dined on filet mignon. He also remembered the cross that lit up every evening on the top of the mountain.

To his great embarrassment Teddy had wet the bed on this visit, causing his Aunt Lillian to comment to his uncle that he might be bright but was obviously socially retarded and probably going to grow up to be a pansy. He had wondered at the time whether she intended him to overhear her comment, pronounced after he had gone to bed but was not yet asleep. Years later, she expressed amazement when she heard of his engagement to Melanie; she attended their wedding in an elegant outfit and gave them a set of twelve sterling coffee spoons from Birks on Phillips Square.

Teddy had arranged to spend his last night in Montreal with Piers and Thérèse. He was to meet them for dinner at l'Express, a restaurant on rue St-Denis that Piers told him was part of the Montreal experience. Piers had promised to bring his uncle Norman, a semi-retired music critic and something of a bon vivant. Norman had bought and restored a house in the Vieux-Port which had belonged to a prominent Québécois family, as part of an ongoing project to restore the most memorable buildings of the Old City.

Teddy arrived early at the restaurant and watched the clientele: actors in carefully devised outfits making entrances, chic young women in sequins and lamé embraced by distinguished grey-haired businessmen or politicians, older women in pearls and chiffon showing off their younger escorts in black jeans and leather jackets. Piers arrived alone half an hour late. He explained that Thérèse had a headache and his uncle Norman was indisposed. He could only stay for an hour. Teddy ordered a second martini and *steak tartare*. Piers ordered a beer and *frites*. They sat looking at each other while the beau monde of Montreal swirled around them. Teddy expected Piers to make some witty remark such as he would have in the old days, but he seemed preoccupied. He told Teddy he'd just heard from his son in Vancouver who needed money to fly home. He'd been convicted of drunken driving and had spent the previous night in jail. Teddy thought he could add a few stories about some of his own children's misadventures: how he had kicked his eldest son out of the house, or more accurately the residence in Lima, saying, "You're not going to sit at home all day blowing dope," or how he had dissuaded his daughter from marrying an Egyptian taxi driver, but thought better of it.

After Piers left, Teddy decided to walk back to his hotel. He stopped on Prince Arthur to watch the buskers and magicians and fire-eaters. He found a nearby café and ordered a coffee. The waiter smiled at him. "*Avec C ou GM?*" Teddy had forgotten that in Montreal he could order his coffee spiked for a slightly higher price.

The next morning, Teddy had breakfast in the Ritz, then left his bag with the concierge. He walked along Sherbrooke until he came to the corner of Bishop Street. He couldn't resist looking for Sylvain's shop. It was easily found among the many boutiques. He stood outside it for a minute, then opened the door and walked in. The shop was full of arrow-backed chairs, diamond-fronted cabinets, pewter candlesticks and tankards, old weather vanes, primitive paintings. Out of a door at the back of the shop came a willowy young man with long jet-black hair. Teddy noticed his shirt was open almost to the waist revealing a firm, muscular stomach.

"*Bonjour. Je peux vous aider?*"

"*Je cherche M. Lemieux.*"

The young man called out, "Sylvain. *Quelqu'un vous visite.*" Sylvain appeared. He smiled at Teddy.

"I wanted to see your shop. And to thank you."

"My pleasure. This is Jean-Marc."

"Your partner?"

"My assistant. He is studying to be a priest. Will I see you again?"

"I'm going to my new post in Jakarta in a few days." He had a sudden thought. "Why don't you come and visit me? You might pick up some interesting curios."

"I might just do that. Gilles is quite capable of running this place without me."

"I'll give you my card. Now I must go."

Sylvain hugged Teddy and kissed him on the mouth. The young man smiled at Teddy and gave him a knowing wink.

As Teddy rode in his cab to the airport, he felt a warm glow, part satisfaction, part anticipation. He thought of the shining cross on the mountain that had excited his imagination years ago. It made him think that somehow Montreal must be closer to heaven than his native Toronto.

THE BISHOP'S VISITOR

Tony Shawcross sat in his study, reading a new book suggesting the historical Christ was actually two people — an idea he found amusing and novel, but highly implausible. His secretary interrupted him to announce a visitor named Mimi. He couldn't put a face to the name, although the visitor claimed to know him.

He asked that she be shown in. When the woman appeared in the doorway, he stood up. She was small, painfully thin, and looked to be about seventy-five years old. She had snow-white hair and wore neither makeup nor jewellery. Her faded, rust-coloured pantsuit seemed several sizes too big.

"You don't remember me, eh? Trinity College chapel, 1957."

"Molly Godwin."

"The same."

She held out a slender, heavily veined hand. He took it gingerly in his much larger one and asked her to sit down. She smiled suddenly and settled into a leather-covered wingback chair.

Her smile opened a shaft of memory. It was the smile she had sometimes flashed at him when they were cast in a student production of T. S. Eliot's *Murder in the Cathedral*, she as the leader of the chorus of Women of Canterbury, he as the Fourth Tempter. She had had some training as a dancer and devised swirling choreography for the Canterbury women; she also coached them in the articulation of their lines. As their physical mobility and choral work were inevitably somewhat ragged, she ended up dancing alone and speaking many of the lines as a solo in her richly sonorous voice with its slightly British inflections.

The young director had devised surprise entrances for some members of his cast. This necessitated Molly and Tony spending twenty minutes each night alone together in the tiny vestry while the audience filed in. There wasn't room for chairs; they sat on the stone floor. Tony, who played soccer but was not really an athletic type, marvelled at Molly's suppleness as she sat cross-legged or hugged her knees up under her chin.

She smoked in the vestry, two or three cigarettes in their twenty-minute wait, hitching up her floor-length skirts to reveal a silver flask of whisky strapped to her thigh. He always turned down her offers to share a cigarette; he was afraid the smell would be detected, but it was apparently covered by the incense used in chapel services. He did once accept a swallow of amber liquid that burned all the way down to his gut.

He also discovered one day, when she demonstrated a cartwheel, that she wore no underpants. When questioned, she insisted she needed to be free to move. None of the other men in the cast were present for this display. Tony hoped none of the women in the chorus spread the word about Molly's lack of underpinnings. If the chaplain were to hear of it, he would demand they cancel the performance. Tony remembered Molly had a much fuller figure then, with sizeable breasts that bounced teasingly under her tight sweater at rehearsals. Eventually, he got up the courage to ask her to a formal dance, but she was committed to go with someone else. "Perhaps next year?" she'd offered. But the following year she was gone.

And now here she was in his office, once more sitting cross-legged, looking about seventy-five. Could she be that old? He was sixty-three. He had been a second-year divinity student of twenty-four and she was in her first year of arts, so probably no more than eighteen, which would mean she must be about fifty-six or -seven. What had she done to age so drastically? He was too tactful to bring up the subject. Instead he said, "It's wonderful to see you again after all these years. Of course I've seen you on television."

"The last few years I've made a specialty of old hags. I often play the mother of someone ten years older than I am." She grimaced and lit a cigarette. Although it had been forbidden to smoke in the church offices long before it was banned in all public buildings, Tony raised no objection. He found an ashtray in one of the drawers of his desk and offered it to her.

"You changed your name to Mimi."

"It's what my brothers called me, because I could speak French. I spent a year in a convent in Quebec before I went to Branksome, which I look back on as the worst time in my life. I was head girl and captain of the ground hockey team. Frightfully bouncy and jolly. Horrible."

"You stayed only one year at Trinity?"

"An aspiring filmmaker saw me in *Murder*, offered me a part in a movie he was shooting in Montreal. My career took off. I loved Montreal. I learned some expressions I'd never heard from the nuns." Her laugh was husky and sensual.

"You're not still living in Montreal?"

"I took my earnings from *Breton Trail* and bought an old farmhouse in the Languedoc, where I spend my time when I'm not working. I've just sold it."

"You won't miss it?"

"It was time."

"But you still work?"

"Last week I finished a movie with that Australian who's so hot now."

"Paul ... what's-his-name?"

"That's right. Paul What's-his-name. I fucked him. He has a tiny dick."

Tony was reminded that in an effort not to seem too "wet and weedy," in the parlance of the era, he had recited for her benefit a slightly off-colour limerick:

> *There was a young woman of Chichester*
> *Who made all the saints in their niches stir.*
> *One morning at matins*
> *Her breasts beneath satins*
> *Made the Bishop of Chichester's britches stir.*

She quickly countered with an ecclesiastical limerick of her own:

> *There was a young lady of Crewe*
> *Who said as the curate withdrew,*
> *"The vicar is quicker*
> *And slicker and thicker*
> *And two inches longer than you."*

She responded to this memory with another laugh that ended in a rasping cough. He poured her a glass of water, which she gulped down gratefully.

"I could offer you something stronger. Whisky? I seem to remember that was your tipple."

"Thank you, no. I'm a recovering alcoholic. In fact I've just come from an AA meeting."

He suddenly remembered a warm Montreal afternoon when he had played hooky from a boring conference. He was sitting in a sidewalk café on rue St-Denis when he caught sight of a figure coming towards him. She had blue hair, a very short yellow miniskirt, black and green striped leotards, and was tottering along in high-heeled wedgies. In spite of her bizarre get-up there was something familiar about her. Could it have been Molly? He had got to his feet, intending to greet her. She turned her ankle and staggered as she recovered her balance. He had wondered if she might be drunk. In his moment of hesitation, the woman was greeted by a friend, a young man with shoulder-length hair. She turned towards him and Tony realized she was in the last months of pregnancy.

Tony was aware he had left a gap in their conversation; he quickly asked, "You had a child, didn't you? An actor, too?"

"No, thank God. He's a chef with his own very successful restaurant in Whistler. I married his father shortly after he was born, but I wasn't any good at family life."

"You still see him?"

"My son? Yes. He has two little girls who are rather sweet, although I don't much like spending time with young children."

"My children were crazy about the character you played on *Breton Trail*. You were so funny and yet pathetic. We watched it every Sunday night for years."

"It's nice to know I gave some people pleasure. My life has been rather a mess in many ways. I think I experimented with too many things ... and people."

"But you've kept going."

"Until now. I'm here to discuss my funeral. I'd like you to conduct it."

"I'm flattered," he managed to respond.

"I want my two favourite hymns: 'Praise, my Soul, the King of Heaven' and 'To be a Pilgrim.' I want a boys' choir and candles and you must wear your full fig: mitre, crozier, the works. I'm a sucker for spectacle."

"That could all be arranged."

"I've been working at the Salvation Army hostel down the street. All the staff and inmates want to attend. I hope that's all right."

"Of course." He prided himself on being ecumenical.

"I'd suggest you hold it on a Wednesday afternoon. It's a matinee day. Not too many actors will be able to attend. On no account are any actors to be allowed to speak."

"I assume you've been confirmed?"

"Oh, yes. At school. I have my own faith. I'm not too sure about that Jesus guy, though he had some good ideas."

Tony smiled. "You're not alone there."

"I can't fix an actual date but it will be soon. I have terminal cancer. The doctors have given me about three weeks." She smiled brightly. "I still love limericks. Here's one I made up recently:

> *There was a musician from Sparta*
> *Who was a prodigious farter.*
> *He could blow out his ass*
> *The B minor mass*
> *And for an encore* La Traviata.*"

Tony couldn't help laughing.

Molly stood up. "When we were alone in the vestry I always hoped you were going to surprise me with a kiss. This is your last chance." She turned her face towards him. He closed his eyes and for a moment he saw her as she had been at the age of eighteen. He moved towards her, took her wrinkled face in his hands, and their lips met. Her mouth was open. It was the most passionate kiss he had experienced in years.

He watched as she turned and walked fully erect through the doorway and out of his office. Surprised at his own unexpected emotion he sat at his desk and poured himself a glass of whisky. This time it didn't burn his throat; it steadied him and helped him regain his customary composure.

WRITER'S BLOCK

Frank Connacher sat in the bar of The Pilot and ordered his second double whisky. There was a copy of the newspaper, his newspaper, on the counter. He resisted the urge to tear it into tiny pieces.

Ted, the bartender, looked down on him. "You don't look too chipper today."

"I'm not."

Ted waited for an explanation but it was not forthcoming. "I thought you'd given up coming here."

"So did I." Frank thought back on his early days as a writer, when his first collection of poetry had won a prize of five hundred dollars. He read at the Bohemian Embassy surrounded by youthful admirers. It was there he met Johanna, an aspiring novelist. They began a stormy relationship: dinners at Old Angelo's, holding hands across the checkered red tablecloths by the light of a single candle stuck in a straw-based Chianti bottle, followed by a walk through the falling snow to his one-room pad on the third floor of an old house on Gerrard Street, where they argued about art and love. Once Johanna had called him an arrogant prick; he'd hit her. He thought she would leave but instead they ended up in bed together. This pattern was repeated with variations for several months until they decided to take off for Paris together.

In Paris, Frank managed to get a job with the *Herald-Tribune*. Johanna, whose French was infinitely better than his, took a degree at the Sorbonne. After a few months she discovered she was pregnant. Frank thought they should go home but Johanna wanted to finish her degree. He also thought they should get married. They wrangled over both issues. After Zoe was born, Johanna agreed to a civil ceremony. They stayed on for the next two years. It was only when Frank was called up for military service that they decided to go back to Canada.

With his experience in Paris Frank was able to land a job as a journalist writing about European politics. Johanna continued her studies, specializing in Québécois literature. She published a novel, which received patronizing reviews, then decided to concentrate on literary criticism. Her first book, comparing aspects of French and English Canadian poetry, was praised; she soon obtained an appointment at Wainwright College as a lecturer, which led to an assistant professorship. She was a lively and popular teacher, challenging and demanding, but essentially positive and interested in her students. One of them went on to become an assistant producer at CBC, where he suggested she audition for a new talk show. She was picked for the job. Immediately her income doubled, surpassing Frank's. They moved to a better apartment in the Annex and began entertaining Johanna's CBC colleagues and some of her high-profile guests. Frank was pleased for her but resentful of her success, though he realized that she was providing him with an opportunity to meet some very interesting and influential people who could be useful to him in his own career.

FRANK TOOK A TAXI home from The Pilot. He was used to travelling in taxis paid for by the paper. He thought ruefully that he would have to get used to using public transport. He certainly wouldn't be able to afford his own car. In his messy apartment he sat in front of the TV without turning it on. He poured himself another generous shot of whisky and, before long, dozed off. The whisky glass fell onto the frayed carpet.

He was still asleep when the doorbell rang, and he only dimly heard it. He opened his eyes to find his daughter Zoe standing over him. He stared at her bleakly. "Hello, pet." He tried to pull himself out of the chair.

"Don't get up." She sat across from him. "You don't look too good."

"Neither do you."

"Yes, well ... I went to Martha's installation as suffragan bishop."

"I suppose your mother was there."

"She didn't recognize me. Martha brought her over to say hello. I suppose she thought it her Christian duty to instigate a reconciliation. She tried to hug me. I backed off. 'You deserted us,' I said and walked away."

Frank remembered the day he came back from the office to find Johanna's letter, in which she explained she had fallen in love with another man. He was hurt and angry, even more so when he learned that the other man was a former student of hers and at least nine years her junior. Frank conceded that their early passion had faded, but they had seemed compatible enough. Their work was mutually supportive, even if Johanna had become the brighter star in the media firmament. And what about Zoe? Surely Johanna felt some responsibility to their child. When he learned that Johanna and her new paramour were moving to Paris for a year, she with a leave of absence from the CBC, he to study at the Conservatoire, he became not only bitter but vindictive. They left without a single phone call. Before long, Zoe began receiving letters from her mother in Paris. Prompted by Frank, she returned them unopened.

Frank picked up the empty whisky glass and poured himself a healthy shot from the bottle sitting beside it. He emptied the glass in two gulps.

Zoe gave him a sharp look. "Something the matter?"

Frank said nothing.

Zoe went into her father's kitchen, where she rinsed and stacked the dirty dishes. She peered into the refrigerator, throwing out mouldy dishes of leftovers. She whipped up an omelette with bits of ham and red pepper and a few soggy mushrooms, which she hoped would be tasty enough when cooked. There was no hope of making an edible salad but she found some bread, best if toasted. She set the table, found some reasonably clean napkins, helped Frank out of his chair and propelled him to the table. She set the omelette in front of him. He toyed with it, not wanting to hurt her feelings.

"Why don't you tell me what's the matter?"

"They've let me go."

"The newspaper? Just like that?"

"They've got to cut costs. I still get to do one column a week. Thank God I've paid your first-term fees."

"I'll get a job."

"You should finish your degree."

Zoe got up and carried the dirty dishes into the kitchen. She washed them and put them away. When she went back into the living room, Frank was sitting in his easy chair with a fresh glass of whisky. He tried to smile but the prospect that in a month his livelihood would be cut in half was depressing. He had pointed out to his editor that he had been on staff with the paper for more than twenty years; the editor responded that he was lucky he was not being laid off altogether. Maybe Frank could get some freelance work with a magazine. But the magazines were in trouble as well and Frank couldn't see himself churning out the sort of glib material they were looking for. "What about your own writing? You'll have more time for that," the editor said cheerily. Frank's last collection of short stories had netted him less than two thousand dollars in royalties and he hadn't been able to get it reviewed in his own paper.

Zoe kissed him on the brow. "Got to go." She headed for the door. Zoe was in her third year of medical school, but she had at least three more years before she would earn anything as a resident. She would undoubtedly want to be a specialist. How was he going to finance this?

TWO DAYS LATER, FRANK had a call from Martha. She had been a close friend of Johanna's since their college days and a frequent guest at the dinner parties Frank and Johanna gave when they were still together. Although she was one of the first women to become an Anglican priest, she was not straitlaced and stuffy; in fact she had a lively sense of humour that often bordered on the bawdy. After the split she stayed in touch with Frank, understanding that he could probably use some moral support, though she refrained from criticizing Johanna, more because she did not want to be caught in the crossfire than out of any sense of loyalty to her old friend. She invited Frank to have lunch with her at the York Club; after a brief hesitation, he agreed.

"Will you be wearing your new mitre?"

Martha chuckled. "They have a rather strict dress code. You do have a suit and tie?"

They sat in the garden. A waiter in a tailcoat offered them a choice of champagne or Chablis. Frank thought he might as well make the most of the opportunity and opted for champagne.

Martha came straight to the point. "Zoe came to my installation. She's such a pretty girl. And so bright. I think she'll make a wonderful doctor."

"If I can afford to keep her in school."

"I heard you'd lost your job. Zoe told me."

"She had no business doing that."

"I'm her godmother. It's only natural for her to share her worries with me. I could help pay for the rest of her schooling. And I think Johanna would also like to contribute."

"No way."

"I can understand your reluctance. But if it's a question of the girl's future …"

"Even if I agreed, Zoe wouldn't."

"I think you should talk to Zoe about the possibility."

"Is it my Christian duty?"

Martha looked at him for a long moment. "It's an option. I think you should let Zoe decide."

There was silence until the steward arrived with their cold poached salmon. Martha turned the conversation to a discussion of recent films she had seen; she'd always been something of a movie buff. He hadn't seen any of the films she mentioned, but deplored the fact that most recent Hollywood films were nothing but sex and violence.

"Oh, don't be such an old stick, Frank. I thoroughly enjoyed *Lord of the Rings* and *Pirates of the Caribbean.* I think you would too. You need to get out more. Take your mind off your troubles. I want you to come with me to see the new Judi Dench movie this weekend. Promise."

Frank gave her a smile that was more grimace than anything and reluctantly agreed. He didn't want her solicitude, though he appreciated her good intentions.

FRANK WENT THROUGH HIS files and came up with a few articles he had written that had been rejected or accepted but not printed: an interview with a successful Canadian novelist now living in London; a piece about the ties of a Montreal developer to the Sicilian mafia; a piece about salmon fishing in the Highlands with a Scottish earl; an account of a weekend spent in Jerez where he had met Don Felipe, the head of a family that had produced sherry for over two hundred years. The Don had a passion for training horses in the art of dressage and had set up a replica of the Spanische Hofreitschule in Vienna.

Frank decided to call on four magazine editors he knew. Longtime friends, they all agreed to see him. In the old days they would have taken him to lunch at La Maquette or Canoe, high above the city in the Toronto Dominion tower. Now they kept him waiting for half an hour in their outer offices and signalled the end of the interview after fifteen minutes. He did manage to sell one story to a lifestyle magazine; it was about the experience of a friend who had bought and fixed up an old farmhouse in the Dordogne. The sale was contingent upon a reduction from two thousand words to eight hundred. He understood he was to be paid by the word and he would have to hound the editor for payment.

Frank was sitting at his computer in his pyjamas, a glass of whisky beside him. He hadn't shaved or been outside for three days. He was working on his Friday column; it was not going well. He reached for the glass when the doorbell rang. He decided to ignore it but the ringer was persistent. He shambled to the door and was confronted by Johanna in a smart pinstripe suit. "May I come in? I need to talk to you."

"After twenty years? You must want something."

She shrugged and pushed her way past him into the living room. She cleared a patch for herself on the sofa and sat down, stretching her long legs out in front of her. "I hear the paper has let you go. Martha told me. I might be able to get you something at the CBC."

"In return for what?"

"I'd like to take over paying for Zoe's university fees."

"You'll have to talk to her about that. She's still very bitter. You left her."

"I fell in love."

He didn't reply. He looked at his estranged wife, so assured and confident. She believed she could solve any problem, handle any difficulty. This was not new, and years of success had only reinforced her belief in herself. It was not that she believed she was always right — she was open to other opinions, especially if she could co-opt them and use them to her advantage. She had such a firm grip on her own identity that she saw no harm in absorbing new ideas or even changing her positions radically.

She looked across at him levelly. "I have another proposition." She paused. He waited. "This is strictly confidential. I am about to be offered the position of Master of St. Augustine College. The first woman Master."

"Congratulations. But shouldn't your title be Mistress? I'm sure St. Augustine must have had some. Why else would he have written his *Confessions*?"

"You know we've never been divorced. I wondered whether you would be interested in taking up your role as my husband."

Frank looked at her incredulously.

"You'd meet some very interesting people. We wouldn't have to live together. You could just appear at functions with me."

"Don't you have a current paramour?"

"He's not interested in being associated with me in public."

"Why not?"

"I'd rather not go into it. Will you at least think it over?"

Frank said nothing. Johanna got up. "How do I get in touch with Zoe?"

"I can give you the number of her cellphone."

He wrote it out on a scrap of paper and handed it to her.

"Thank you. I must be going." She moved towards the door.

"I will hear from you?"

Frank sat down. The sheer unadulterated gall of the woman. He could use her help, but he couldn't imagine lowering himself to accept it. As for Zoe, Johanna would be lucky if the girl didn't hang up on her. But he felt he had no right to deprive her of her mother's proffered assistance. He thought of calling and warning her, but then thought better of it. The girl was strong enough to look out for herself.

A FEW DAYS LATER, Frank received a phone call from a CBC producer asking him to come to his office for a meeting. He shaved and put on a clean shirt and tie. He realized when he was ushered into the producer's office that he needn't have bothered. The producer had three days' growth of beard and was wearing a Maple Leafs hockey sweater. Sitting across from him was an attractive woman. Frank judged her to be in her early forties. She was wearing a multi-coloured blouse, an embroidered Mexican skirt, and huge hoop earrings. She was overweight but had a pretty face.

The producer smiled at him encouragingly. "I've been reading your columns for years." He paused. "I understand you might be interested in doing some work for us. I remember you did some pieces about the mafia in Montreal and Toronto and their ties with Sicily and Calabria. Would you be willing to tackle that subject in, let us say, three one-hour documentaries? You would have to get some interviews. And it would be for radio, you understand."

"I suppose I could have a shot at it."

"Excellent. Gloria here will be your producer. She's fluent in Italian."

"I'm fluent in Spanish," Gloria corrected him. "I can manage."

"We'd like an outline. One or two pages for each program. If we accept your proposal, we'll draw up a contract. One third in advance, one third upon completion of the edit, and the final third when broadcast. I'm afraid we can only pay you scale."

Gloria smiled at Frank. "I'm really looking forward to working with you."

The producer stood up and proffered his hand. Frank left the office and went downstairs to the cafeteria. He ordered an Americano and watched people coming and going, laughing and gossiping. Obviously Johanna expected some sort of payback.

Frank went back to his files. He had copies of most of his mafia columns. He would have to persuade his contacts to be interviewed. It would be harder to convince them if they knew their voices were going to be heard on air. Fortunately, he had kept tapes of some of his interviews when he wrote the series of articles. He wasn't sure if they were broadcast quality, but he would take them to Gloria and let her be the judge. He sat down and began to work on his outlines. He felt invigorated to have a new project and was able to turn out what he considered a good presentation. He had learned to work quickly as a journalist and, although he was not an accomplished typist, working on a computer allowed him to correct his mistakes and move copy around quickly.

That Sunday he went to the movies with Martha. The film was about elderly Brits on holiday at a hotel in India and although he thought it a bit silly he found it amusing. He took Martha to supper afterwards in a small Indian restaurant. He had wondered whether he should tell her about Johanna's visit, but decided against it. Martha informed him that Johanna's appointment as Master of St. Augustine had been confirmed and that her new book *The Myth of Christ* had won a prestigious prize in England. Frank hadn't realized Johanna had moved from the field of literary criticism to theology after she was ordained as an Anglican priest eight years ago. Martha also informed him that she had spoken with Zoe and offered her an interest-free loan if she needed it. Zoe had said she would think about it. "She seems very level-headed. She's a credit to you, Frank."

This comment pleased Frank, but he merely smiled acknowledgement as he sipped his brandy.

On Monday morning he phoned Gloria and set up an appointment to meet in her office. She offered him coffee, which he sipped while she read his outlines and marked them up. "It's a bit thin. I think you should explore the early history of the mafia more thoroughly. I'm sure you can find material on the Internet. And you need to sum up your conclusions at the end more succinctly. But with a few changes I think the second and third episodes are almost there."

She then offered to listen to his tapes, which she fed into an old-style machine in an office down the hall. She smiled at him encouragingly. "I think we can salvage some of it," she said, continuing to smile. "We've got a lot of work ahead of us. I wonder if we could get permission to use some sound bites from *The Godfather*. I'll check that out. You'd better e-mail me your corrected outlines as quickly as you can. We're meeting Wednesday morning to discuss the schedule for the next six months." Frank went home and got to work. Gloria's brisk but positive manner had energized him and given him confidence.

On Tuesday evening Zoe showed up. She had bought a pizza. While it was warming in the oven, she sat opposite him and gave him a quizzical look. "Johanna called me yesterday. I wondered how she got my cell number."

"I gave it to her. Martha convinced me you should make your own decision."

"She offered to pay my university fees. I told her to go jump in the lake and hung up. It's totally outrageous. She thinks she can buy me off after neglecting me for twenty years."

"She set it up for me to get some work at the CBC."

"And you accepted?"

"I need the work. And I like the producer they've assigned to me."

Zoe admitted that this was a good thing. She brought the pizza to the table from the oven and they ate in silence. Frank wondered if he should tell her about the rest of Johanna's offer, but decided against it. No sense stoking the fire. Zoe took the dishes to the kitchen and once again cleaned up what was in the sink. She was relieved to see that the kitchen seemed tidier and that there were fewer empty whisky bottles lying around.

"I've managed to get a part time job working in a lab."

"Will you have time for that?"

"I'll manage. The pay's not great, but it'll help. And Martha's offered to make me a loan if I need it. She told me you two were dating on the sly."

"We went to a movie together."

"Just kidding." She said her goodbyes and left.

FRANK ENJOYED WORKING WITH Gloria. She was deft and decisive without seeming to be controlling. They made their way through the material Frank brought in, discarding some bits and trimming others. She would sometimes suggest a different slant or a new source of material, but was always willing to listen to his ideas. She had a ready sense of humour and they laughed a good deal. Frank was not an early riser and rarely made it into her office before eleven, but this didn't seem to bother her. They sometimes worked into the evenings. One night they went to the Kit Kat club on King Street for a late dinner. They had lobster ravioli and demolished a bottle of Orvieto Classico. Frank was about to order a brandy when Gloria surprised him. "I'd ask you to my place for a nightcap," she said, "but I live in the Beaches and I have a fourteen-year-old who might not approve. He can be very judgmental."

"I didn't realize you were a mom."

"Oh, yes."

"You could come to my place. It's not that far away."

She immediately suggested they take a cab.

Back at his flat he offered her Scotch. He had no soda and he had forgotten to refill the ice trays but she seemed perfectly content to drink it neat. He put on a record, Ella Fitzgerald singing Cole Porter. He turned around to find her sitting on the floor, leaning against the sofa, her ample skirt pulled up enough to reveal her still-shapely legs. He sat on the sofa and looked down on her.

"You're divorced?"

"Never married. Blake is a love child. I went on a holiday to Guatemala with a married man. When I told him I was pregnant he told me he wanted no involvement with a child and offered to pay for an abortion. I told him to fuck off. I'm not sorry. Blake is a good kid. But now he wants to know who his father is. At first I told him I didn't know. Now I ... just don't know. What do you think?"

"I have a daughter who's completely estranged from her mother. Partly my doing. She deserted us and I was very angry. Now I'm sorry. Her mother's ruthlessly ambitious but gifted and successful. Zoe's halfway through medical school and her mother has offered to help her financially. I'd hate to see her pile up a huge debt in student loans."

Gloria leaned her head against Frank's knee. He swirled his whisky in his glass and downed it. Then he slid off the sofa and sat beside her on the floor. She turned her face to him, waiting to be kissed.

The next morning when he woke up he could hear her

humming in the kitchen. He pulled on his underpants and a shirt and trousers and made his way into the living room where she had laid out some plates and cutlery. She brought him toast and coffee and sat across from him.

"I enjoyed that. It's been quite a while."

"For me too." In fact he hadn't been at all sure he could manage to get it up but Gloria had been patient and accommodating.

"Don't worry. I'm not expecting any permanent commitment." She finished her coffee and stood up. "I'm going to the office. I'll expect you sometime before noon."

Frank wondered if he had looked worried. He was relieved by her statement on one level but realized he had been hoping that this was just the beginning.

In the weeks that followed they slept together several times. Gloria told him that she had made a decision to arrange a meeting between Blake and his father, who was delighted to find he had a bright, good-looking son he hadn't had the trouble of bringing up. She also told Blake she had a new boyfriend and he accepted this without hostility. She thought perhaps his newfound relationship with his dad compensated for her diminished attention and more frequent absences from home.

WHEN MARTHA PHONED FRANK a few weeks later to ask him if he would accompany her to Johanna's installation she was surprised to find that he was willing, provided he could bring a friend. This was fine with her; she didn't pry into who the friend might be. That same day Zoe dropped in on him. Martha had asked her as well, and she had firmly declined. She was surprised to learn that her father was willing to go. She had not seen him for nearly a month because of her new job. She reported that she was quite enjoying it, but the work and her studies left her little time for anything else. She thought Frank looked better and certainly the apartment was less messy. He told her about his work at the CBC, though not about Gloria. She attributed his more cheerful outlook to this new interest and was happy for him.

The day of Johanna's installation was bright with a sharp nip in the autumn air. The Eucharist was held in the college's neo-Gothic chapel, from which the academics processed to a suitably capacious auditorium nearby, wearing gowns with splendidly coloured hoods of crimson, indigo, purple, and gold and square tasselled or flat black velvet caps. The ceremony was long and boring. Frank thought Gloria might want to leave before it was over, but she stuck it out. Afterwards there was a reception in the Great Hall with wine and canapés. Johanna was surrounded by well-wishers. Martha came over to where Frank and Gloria were standing, a female journalist in tow. Frank recognized Margaret Frisbee — a sharp investigator who loved a good story.

"You must be very proud of your wife, Frank."

"She's got what she wanted."

"You're not still living with her?"

"We haven't spoken for twenty years. She deserted me and our daughter. I think it was because I failed to get a job on a TV show called *This Hour is a Week*. She thought I was a loser."

Margaret gave him a look. "Obviously you won't want to be photographed with her." Frank shrugged.

Margaret beckoned to a photographer. They pushed their way through to Johanna. Frank put his arm around Gloria and waited until Johanna turned towards them. Her smile faded as she took in the couple with a look of astonishment, then she smiled for the camera.

REUNION

Peter turned his seven-year-old Buick onto Revelstoke Drive; he noticed that several monster houses had sprung up on the street, houses with turrets and cupolas, fronted by heraldic lions and large pots full of coleus and begonias and feathery grasses. At the end of the street there was the dense, untended wood he remembered. He swung into the drive and parked beside the dirty Volkswagen van. Before he got his small duffle bag out of the trunk, Benedict appeared on the flagstone steps, bald, slightly stooped, and smiling the same mischievous smile Peter remembered from their college days. He welcomed Peter and led him into the house, where he immediately offered him a drink.

"Wine," Peter said. "Whatever you've got open."

"Most of our friends only drink wine now. I've had a bottle of Chivas for three months and never opened it."

"Ah well, we've done our share to support the Scottish

distillers. It's up to the young now. To them from failing hands we throw the flask. Mmm, this is rather good. Where's it from?"

"Argentina." Benedict, whose last posting had been as ambassador to Chile, favoured South American wines, which he imported by the case. The cabernet Peter was drinking was excellent: full-bodied with a fruity aftertaste of apricots.

"Elizabeth's well?"

"A damn sight more energetic than I am. She's doing a final shop for tonight. We're supplying the main course and the wine. Alice Wainwright is making a dessert. Dickie is bringing the hors d'oeuvre."

"Can I do anything?"

"Just be your inimitable self. There's a certain amount of curiosity about you. After nearly fifty years."

"On my part, too. I wonder how many I'll recognize. I won't know many of the wives."

"There'll be more wives than husbands. Cosette, Boris's widow. We didn't know what to do about Andrew."

"You could have consulted the Chief of Protocol."

"In the end, we asked both his wives. They were both at the funeral. Lucy's remarried, but she's not bringing her new husband. He's some sort of scientist and apparently has no small talk."

"He could try us on big talk."

Elizabeth appeared in the doorway, loaded down with shopping bags. "Benedict, did you get the balsamic vinegar?" Her voice was shrill from years of trying to bring order to the chaotic lives of her husband and four sons. Benedict regarded this as an amusing foible and their boys followed his example, which only encouraged Elizabeth to strive harder towards her patently impossible goal.

"Our first guest has arrived."

"Hello, old thing." She clung to the affected private-schoolgirl Anglicisms of her youth, but offered both cheeks to be kissed. Peter remembered that when he was a junior in External this ritual had seemed an exotic, European courtesy. Now every suburban housewife affected it.

"Lovely to see you, Elizabeth. You look splendid." Peter was genuinely fond of Elizabeth. He knew she didn't receive many compliments, and in spite of her determined shunning of feminine wiles — no makeup, no fancy hair styling, only a clunky ethnic necklace bought to support a worthy cause in Guatemala — she still had a pretty face. Her slight flush betrayed her pleasure at Peter's attention. She shrilled at Benedict as she headed to the kitchen with her purchases.

"Did you make the carrot salad?"

"It's in the fridge."

"There's peel all over the floor. We do have a garbage pail."

"I'll clean it up."

"Stay out of my kitchen. You've made enough mess. But I need the vinegar for the tomatoes."

"It's on the counter. I got a special new kind from Provence."

"I didn't tell you to buy a gallon. There's enough here to keep a restaurant going for six months. Forty-eight dollars! Are you out of your mind?"

"It's my contribution. We won't charge it to expenses for the party."

"Well, it's not coming out of my housekeeping money."

"Another glass of wine, Peter?"

"I think I'd like to go upstairs and put my feet up if you don't mind. If I don't reappear in half an hour, give me a wake-up call."

Like the rest of the house, the room Peter was assigned was full of pre-Columbian artifacts. Benedict's first posting had been Mexico. Peter had visited Benedict and Elizabeth there and had travelled with them and their four sons in a station wagon to obscure Mexican towns that specialized in making pottery, blankets, carved animals, silver jewellery, masks, straw hats, exotic liqueurs, rebozos, and serapes. Benedict bought quantities of all these items; he wore the hats and serapes, filled the kitchen with cooking pots, and covered the walls with masks and primitive paintings. His subsequent postings in Israel, Indonesia, Japan, and Argentina gave him ample opportunity to build a respectable collection of primitive art. When he was home in Canada he augmented the small selection of Inuit carvings and prints he had started before he left Ottawa. Elizabeth railed and groaned in protest, which only egged him on to further acquisitions. Recently he had returned from supervising elections in Mali, laden with masks, drums, and printed cotton — accompanied by a twenty-two-year-old student who he offered to put up while he went to university.

Peter had known Benedict longer than Elizabeth. He had

been a day boy at the private school where Benedict was a boarder. Although Peter had been two years his junior, he and Benedict shared an interest in history and debating. At college, they were part of the same debating team that visited several eastern Canadian universities and usually won. After his final year, Benedict invited Peter to go to Greece with him and stay with his parents. His father was the Canadian ambassador and they lived in splendour in a fine old house just north of Athens. Together they visited the ruins at Knossos and took a freighter to Istanbul. They sailed the Bosphorus at dawn and saw the minarets of Hagia Sophia and the Blue Mosque silhouetted against the pink-streaked morning sky. Benedict went on to Oxford, while Peter completed his undergraduate degree. Benedict wrote, urging him to sit the entrance exams for External; almost as a dare, Peter did. To everyone's amazement, including his own, he was accepted and became the youngest foreign service officer in the Department's history.

Peter awoke at six-fifteen and jumped up off the bed. He went into the bathroom, brushed his teeth, and spattered cold water on his face and torso. He put on a clean shirt, decided against wearing a tie, but put on his light cotton jacket. He went downstairs where Elizabeth was setting out food on the dining-room table, all the while berating Benedict, who had decided at the last moment to take a bath. He was unabashed by her tirade and disappeared upstairs. Peter helped her set out cutlery, napkins, and wine glasses, and fanned out paper cocktail napkins on the coffee table. He set up a bar on the sideboard with ice, lemon wedges, and sparkling water. The doorbell rang and he let in the first arrivals, Dickie Merriweather and his new girlfriend, Andrea.

Dickie had been at college with Peter and although they had not been close friends they had lived on the same floor in residence. Technically, he had been admitted to External a year later than Peter and Benedict, but he had dated Camilla, a woman who had been in their year. When they married, she resigned in accordance with the rules of the time, although it was generally understood she was the more capable officer. Dickie was intelligent, but silly. Too silly to be appointed ambassador, though he eventually became the senior Canadian representative on two different United Nations committees. Camilla died of cancer during his last posting and he took early retirement, though on full pension. He had met Andrea at his wife's funeral; an understanding had taken shape. They lived in separate houses, but went everywhere together. Andrea was bright and aggressive, a journalist and broadcaster who had a weekly cooking show on an Ottawa television station and who also wrote a column about wine in the Life section of the Saturday paper.

"Dickie's made the most divine crab and avocado dip," bellowed Andrea. Dickie was rather deaf, but Peter suspected she had always bellowed. "And I've done a little number with smoked salmon. I had the recipe from the Queen Mother's personal cook."

"And the Queen Mother's personal gillie caught the salmon?"

"Oh, you are naughty, Peter."

The doorbell rang. Peter opened the door and was confronted by two couples. He managed to identify Arthur Wainwright, though he now had a neatly trimmed beard and two hearing aids. "Fifty years on. You look just the same, Peter."

"So do you." A lie, but well-intentioned.

"This is my wife Alice. And you know who this is."

The woman with the walker was pot-bellied and stooped with thinning grey hair that barely covered her scalp.

"Of course he doesn't. I'm Phyllis and this is my husband Tim." Phyllis had been tall, slim, and brisk, with soft chestnut brown hair in a neat Dutch cut. Only the bright blue eyes were still the same.

"Come in, come in." Peter led them into the living room, where Elizabeth was smiling a bit shyly, still in her apron. "Silly old Benedict is still in the bath. Peter, can you get people their drinks?" After the obligatory cheek-kissing all round, a babble set up about how long it had taken to drive in from the Gatineau or Merrickville. These people saw each other fairly regularly. They went on to bring each other up to speed on the progress of their various ailments and the recent exploits and achievements of their grandchildren.

In the dining room, Peter and Dickie fixed drinks. Arthur wanted a Scotch and soda. Alice opted for Campari. Peter filled these special orders while Dickie poured glasses of white wine.

"I don't suppose Norman is coming."

"Nobody's heard from him in years. After he divorced

Helena, he married a Belgian countess, or so we were led to believe. But then everyone in Belgium has a title."

Dickie sailed away with his tray of drinks. Benedict appeared, fresh from his bath, wearing a Mexican wedding shirt. He went off to answer the doorbell and ushered into the living room John Taylor and two of the widows. John was pulling a little oxygen tank on wheels and Cosette was wearing a paisley headscarf to hide the baldness resulting from her radiation treatments. Rita seemed unscathed by the ravages of time, except that her hair was now snow-white. They were ushered into the living room. The doorbell rang again. The entrance of a diminutive but sharp-eyed octogenarian broke through the chatter.

"Gordon. What a lovely surprise," said Phyllis. "I'd stand up in your honour if I could."

"No need. I've shrunk so I'm about the same size as you are sitting down." Gordon Rintoul was unsmiling, but his eyes had a slight twinkle that Peter remembered from the days when he was the Head of Far Eastern Division. He shook hands with Phyllis and turned his head. "So you're Peter Graham. One of the most promising young officers I ever knew — and you left after three years. No regrets?"

"Not really."

"Good. I seem to remember you made a very passable martini?"

"Is that what you found so promising?"

"That was certainly part of it, though I don't believe I mentioned it in my confidential report on you."

"I take it you'd like to see if I've lived up to my potential. Olives or a twist?"

"Olives. I'm sour enough as it is."

Back at the sideboard, Dickie said, "Gordon hasn't changed. I used to find him absolutely terrifying and I still tremble every time he fixes those sharp little eyes on me."

"You were always a sensitive little thing, Dickie. He terrified all of us, even Alastair, though he would never have admitted it."

"I think everyone's here," said Elizabeth. "I'll get the casserole out of the oven."

"What about Lucy?"

"She's probably involved in some sort of good works. She won't mind if we start without her."

The chatter continued as the assembled crowd drifted into the dining room, where they spooned out small portions onto their plates. The women clustered in the living room and sat in groups, talking of winter holiday spots, exchanging notes on cleaning ladies and caterers. The men stood in the dining room and excoriated the follies of George Bush.

"Of course the war is about oil more than anything else, but surely after Vietnam and Russia's experience in Afghanistan they realize that continuing a war they can't win is bound to fatally weaken their economy. They're in debt to China — how many billions?"

"Or trillions? What is a trillion anyway?"

"The Chinese know if anybody does."

"They say China's GDP will equal Britain's this year."

"China's purchasing power will surpass America's this year." Gordon Rintoul was what the British used to call a "China hand." His parents had been missionaries there and he spoke fluent Mandarin. He had been the Canadian Ambassador to both China and Japan. "It's only a matter of time until China gains control of the dollar. With their holdings in American currency and bonds ..."

"And they're embarking on joint military manoeuvres with Russia, even as we speak. There's no question they'll be running the world by mid-century."

"Well, none of us will be around to see it."

"Thank God."

Lucy came into the living room. Her voice was warm, but penetrating. "Sorry I'm late. I've brought a surprise guest. In fact two guests." She was followed by an elegant, smartly dressed woman who everyone immediately recognized as Marie-Josée and a slim, willowy younger woman with Asian features.

"I couldn't resist Lucy's invitation. She's terribly persuasive. And I brought my daughter Chloé."

Marie-Josée and Lucy were greeted with kisses all round. When Marie-Josée got to Peter she smiled. "You look even handsomer."

"You couldn't be improved upon. But age has certainly not withered you."

"Flatterer. Have you been back to Indochina?"

"Yes, about four years ago. Laos has hardly changed at all. Nor Angkor."

PETER RECALLED STEPPING OUT of the helicopter in Siem Reap all those years ago and being greeted by Marie-Josée in a smart white linen dress that set off her splendid neck and shoulders, bronzed by the Cambodian sun. She had managed to commandeer the old French hotel for a meeting of the four Canadian commissioners and their staff. The accommodation was grand and primitive — high ceilings and walls covered with faded brocade — but damp, with sagging mattresses, uncertain plumbing, and sporadic electricity. They gathered on the porch in their tropical whites for cocktails and delicious Cambodian appetizers. Marie-Josée had brought a cook from Phnom Penh.

Peter had flown in from Vientiane with his boss Robert Osborne, a high-spirited man given to sudden changes of mood and scraps both verbal and physical. He and Peter had immediately hit it off. Robert was dismissive of much of the protocol and red tape of External. He sent his dispatches by wire directly to the Minister who had been a friend of his father's and shared his enthusiasm for hockey. Robert admired a small number of the more brilliant senior officers in the Department, but disdained the rest. He was delighted when Peter characterized them as "the Externalia."

Once he arrived in Vientiane, Peter soon realized Robert was simultaneously carrying on an affair with a handsome young woman attached to the Indian delegation and a Thai kick-boxer. He had also established a rapport with several of the Laotian princes in both the Royalist and the Communist factions. He had earned the respect of the Laotians for his sudden, daring missions into the jungle to meet with the rebels, but antagonized both the Indians and Poles by his failure to consult with them on every point of procedure, and the Americans for his far greater knowledge of the political situation and his superior ability to communicate with "the natives."

The meeting in Siem Reap was designed to bring members of the four commissions from North Vietnam, South Vietnam, Cambodia, and Laos together to compare notes and consolidate their efforts. The meetings the next day made it clear that the Vietnamese situation was intractable: the Communists who controlled the north were serious and militarily effective, while the American-supported South Vietnamese regime was weak and corrupt; Emperor Bao Dai was not effective — even as a figurehead. In contrast, Cambodia had the advantage of a charismatic leader in Prince Sihanouk while in Laos the princes heading the rival factions were at least prepared to talk to each other. In fact, Osborne had brokered a tentative deal between them that seemed capable of execution. He therefore emerged as the most successful of the Commissioners and was congratulated by his colleagues — except for Alastair, who, as junior representative from Saigon, prophesied that the Americans would never agree to a settlement that included any participation by Communists.

Alastair was Benedict's older brother. He and Peter had shared an office briefly in the tower of the West Block on Parliament Hill. Tall and handsome in a rangy sort of way, his customary expression was quizzical, not quite a sneer but challenging rather than welcoming. Peter had heard of Alastair, but had never met him before. He and Benedict had gone to different schools; Alastair to Charterhouse rather than Upper Canada, and then the École Pol while Benedict was at Oxford. He was fluent in French, German, and Russian, and had just completed his first year in the Department. Already he was tipped to be posted to Vietnam. Alastair made it clear that he had little or no time for young pups like Peter. His telephone conversations and documents were all in French and he already had a wide acquaintance in the diplomatic corps, which involved a round of cocktail and dinner parties and frequent lunches at the Rideau Club. Peter was not surprised that he had the arrogance to contradict Robert, but wondered how long it would be before Robert struck back.

The day of meetings ended with a visit to the spectacular temples of Angkor. Peter was astonished at their size and grandeur, a virtual equivalent of Versailles in the middle of a tropical jungle. The giant heads cracked open by the invading vegetation, the halls and colonnades decorated with dancing maidens and demons engaged his imagination in a way that the delicate, diminutive palaces of Luang Prabang had not. He climbed the towers and looked out across the surrounding country, where a small procession of worshippers were making their way slowly around the temple, their priests shaded by ceremonial umbrellas, their chants augmented by the honking of long-shafted horns of bone and the ringing of dozens of tiny silver bells. Here for a moment was a glimpse of the old Asia, almost vanished but still intact. Was it in any way connected with the Canadian mission? Probably not; most Cambodians had no idea that an international commission was trying to solve their political problems and shape their future.

The ancient bus that had brought them to the ruins honked its horn and Peter realized it was time for them to go back to the hotel and get ready for what promised to be a splendid dinner, complete with French wines Marie-Josée had somehow managed to have transported from Saigon. On the way down, he stopped to explore one of the corridors and there in a niche he caught a glimpse of a female leg. Another step and he realized it belonged to Marie-Josée. She was seated on a ledge; between her thighs was Alastair, his trousers around his ankles. Peter turned away, hoping they hadn't seen him. He understood then that Marie-Josée had probably organized the whole thing as a way of getting together with Alastair. Peter had heard he was about to marry a Vietnamese girl, but who could be expected to resist the charms of Marie-Josée?

The dinner that night was indeed splendid, and much excellent French wine was consumed. Afterwards, Robert proposed a game of hockey. He provided makeshift sticks and they played in the lobby of the hotel. Peter was on Robert's team and Alastair was on the team of the Commissioner to Cambodia, Jean-Baptiste d'Aubigny-Lantier, an ascetic Quebec aristocrat who proved to be a surprisingly nimble forward. Alastair, though not as deft, was more aggressive. Marie-Josée held her own in their company. They scored two goals before Robert decided to play full out and went after Alastair with a will. Peter knew that this was in retaliation for his remarks in the morning meeting. Robert's team eventually gained a lead and the score stood at three-two when Robert and Alastair got into a fistfight which resulted in a black eye for Alastair and a bloody nose for Robert. D'Aubigny, as the senior officer present, called a halt. They all retired to the terrace for a final brandy.

Peter lingered on the terrace for a last cigarette after most of the others had gone to bed. A full moon shone down on the overgrown garden of the hotel and the silent houses of Siem Reap. Marie-Josée and Alastair appeared and accepted Peter's invitation to join him for a final shot of brandy. Alastair informed Peter that he had got hold of an old Peugeot and that he and Marie-Josée were going to drive back to Phnom Penh together. Peter's efforts to dissuade them were unsuccessful.

"It was Marie-Josée's idea. She dared me. There's no resisting this girl. She's a force of nature."

Peter wished them well as they set off together down the narrow road. He heard their laughter, and then the car revving up and taking off. In spite of himself, he was excited by their reckless passion; it was like a Hollywood movie with Leslie Howard and Merle Oberon.

Two days later, Robert received a telegram from Phnom Penh reporting that Marie-Josée had not arrived. She was missing. Only Peter knew that she had set out with Alastair in the borrowed car. He flew to Phnom Penh and went with one of the military officers in a helicopter to try to find the lost couple. They discovered the Peugeot not far from Siem Reap in two feet of water. Near it, the dead body of Alastair. In the nearest village they found Marie-Josée in the hut of a Cambodian woman. She was bruised and in a state of shock but fully conscious.

She confessed that she had been driving. Alastair was drunk and she had insisted on taking the wheel. She was not used to driving. Alastair continued to harass her until she turned off the road and into the water. Alastair got out and tried to push the car out of the water without success. He got back into the car and began to try to make love to her. She resisted his advances and decided to go back to the road to find help. She got out of the car and Alastair tried to stop her but fell. She kept walking until she reached the village, which was without electricity or telephones but at least provided her with shelter. Peter hesitated. Then he told her they had found Alastair's body. Marie-Josée rolled over on the bed and hid her face. She made no sound, but her shoulders started to heave.

Peter got in touch with d'Aubigny-Lantier, who asked him to stay with Marie-Josée until she could be moved. After two hours, she said she was ready to fly back to Phnom Penh. Peter suggested they leave Alastair's body and come back for it later, but Marie-Josée insisted they bring him with them. Back at the Commission in Phnom Penh, d'Aubigny said he did not want to hear the details. He would simply report that there had been an accident. Diplomats were skilled at suppressing scandal and ignoring irregularities. He would arrange for Marie-Josée to be sent back to Canada and for Alastair's body to be sent to Saigon. Marie-Josée wanted to go to Saigon with it, but d'Aubigny insisted she fly from Bangkok. He asked Peter to go with her and see her safely on the plane.

In spite of her bruises, Marie-Josée appeared for the trip smartly turned out, her eyes hidden behind dark glasses. She obviously didn't want to talk about Alastair and the accident, but exchanged tidbits of diplomatic gossip and reminisced about the absurdities of departmental life in Ottawa. At the Bangkok airport, Peter watched Marie-Josée stride bravely across to the plane and mount the steps of the ladder. At the top she turned, waved, and managed a tiny smile.

Peter returned to Vientiane, where Robert was making plans to close the mission once the negotiations he had initiated were accepted by all parties. But Alastair's prediction proved accurate. The Americans refused to accept a government that had any participation by Communists, no matter how minimal. Robert suffered a bout of malaria, his second, and was invalided home and out of the service, apparently because of his health, although Peter learned later that the real reason was that the Americans had targeted him as a suspected homosexual. His name had appeared on those infamous lists.

Peter returned to Ottawa. He hoped to see Marie-Josée, but she had already been posted to Paris. Before he was offered another posting, he decided to leave the Department. He realized that the real work of the Department was in the hands of a few senior officials and that the rest of them were playing at being diplomats, a pastime slightly more sophisticated than playing house at the age of five but no more related to the real world. As one of the youngest and by no means the brightest of the "Externalia," he could see it would be a long time before he became one of the favoured few doing work of real significance. The utter irrelevance of the work he had done so far depressed him. He had had some fun and learned a few things about working for large organizations, but he was ready to move on. Had this been his third or fourth posting instead of his first he might have understood that much of the work done in any job is irrelevant.

STANDING IN BENEDICT AND Elizabeth's home in Ottawa, surrounded by his contemporaries who had stayed the course, Peter's feelings were unchanged — although he was pleased to observe that they did not seem dissatisfied with their choices. In spite of the superficial bitchiness about politicians and the senior civil servants who had been their masters, they seemed fundamentally good-humoured and continued to take an interest in world affairs. They even had a humorous take on their various ailments. Perhaps constantly adapting to new environments had given them a certain resilience and had helped them to maintain a healthy curiosity.

Gordon Rintoul was reminiscing about an incident involving Robert, when he was first secretary in Washington. He had turned up for a meeting with the Ambassador, who was wearing a pair of sunglasses that failed to hide two black eyes from a barroom quarrel the night before. He was ticked off by the Ambassador for his unseemly appearance and retaliated by exposing one of the Ambassador's comments as completely ungrounded in fact. "He really was a bit of a wild man," said Gordon. "Presumably he became a bit more tactful as the years rolled by."

"Not at all," said Peter. "He continued to show up his superiors for the idiots they often were — even at the CBC, where he went after External. He and his boyfriend continued to get into fights in low-life bars. I rather admired him for that."

"But then you, too, turned out to be a bit of a renegade. That final dispatch you wrote from Vientiane denouncing the cowardice of the Canadian government for not standing up to the Americans. After all, we were only put on the Commission in Indochina to look after the interests of the Americans. That was understood, even by Robert."

"Yes, well, you see where we are after all these years of arse-licking." Peter walked into the kitchen to get another bottle of white wine from the refrigerator. As he was working away with the corkscrew, he saw Marie-Josée standing in the doorway.

"Good old Peter. I'd forgotten what a rebel you could be."

"Might have been if I'd stayed on."

"Regrets?"

"Over the years I've visited some of our former colleagues

as they became senior officers or heads-of-mission, but I never found myself wishing I were in their place. Chloé's charming. And very pretty. She's not married?"

"Oh yes. She has two children."

"You're a grandmother."

"I have seven grandchildren."

"I let Dickie Merriweather speculate that Chloé was the result of an indiscretion between you and some Cambodian prince."

"I've always loved your sense of humour, Peter."

"Are you ready to tell Benedict?"

"I don't know. When I came back here from Phnom Penh, Benedict and Elizabeth were distinctly chilly towards me. Understandably, I suppose."

"I don't think they would be now."

"I'm counting on you to help me. After all, you did talk me into coming here. Please, Peter. A final act of diplomacy."

"This crowd will be clearing out pretty soon. That's one of the great things about entertaining at our age. The guests go home early. You and Chloé stay on."

Peter circulated with the wine, but only one person wanted topping up. Gordon, not surprisingly. The guests soon made their way in small groups to the door and down the path to the driveway. It being late September, the nights were starting to close in, but the sky was still faintly streaked with rose in the west.

"I wonder who'll be around for our sixtieth?"

"Not me, certainly," said Phyllis.

"I'd put money on Lucy."

"Absolutely. It's been great seeing you again, Peter."

"Great for me too. Very encouraging that we're all in such good shape."

"Relatively speaking."

"Yes, well everything's relative, isn't it?"

"Especially in our world. Do come and visit us when you're in Ottawa."

And they were gone. Peter walked back up the path with Benedict. They found Elizabeth and Marie-Josée sitting in the living room. Chloé seemed to have disappeared.

"A real Anglo party. The women sitting in one room, the men standing in another. I'm not a feminist, but ..." Marie-Josée hesitated.

"We could have made them play games. Charades or something," Benedict suggested.

"Made them wear paper hats and given them balloons, perhaps," said Peter. "Marie-Josée has some news for you."

Benedict and Elizabeth looked at Marie-Josée, then back at Peter. In the closing evening air, the silence rested uncomfortably among the old friends.

"Her daughter, Chloé — that is, her adopted daughter, is actually Alastair's daughter. Your brother, Alastair. He had been engaged to a woman in Vietnam. And, well —"

There was a lengthy pause.

"My God, I should have guessed. How stupid of me," said Benedict.

Elizabeth leaned forward. "You're sure of this?"

"Yes," said Marie-Josée. "I got to know her mother. When she died, I adopted Chloé."

Elizabeth cleared her throat. "Why didn't you tell us before?" she asked.

"I wasn't sure how you'd take it. I knew you blamed me for Alastair's death."

"Oh, no. Not really. Alastair was a rascal. We all knew that." Benedict's voice was even, uncompromising.

"But very charming."

"Charm can be fatal."

"As it turned out." Peter regretted this as soon as he said it.

"Goodness, yes." said Elizabeth. "Well, where is Chloé?"

"Chloé …" Marie-Josée called out.

Chloé entered the room from the kitchen. "I was tidying up," she said. She had a slight accent, more French than Asian.

"It turns out I'm your uncle. Did your mother tell you?"

"Yes. I was curious, naturally."

"Well," said Benedict. "Welcome home." He stood up and held out his hands to her. She moved forward and he surrounded her in an awkward embrace. Elizabeth came forward and kissed her. They smiled shyly at each other, like schoolgirls.

"Her home is in Lyon, with her husband and two teenage daughters," said Marie-Josée. "They are very pretty. Like their mother."

Chloé rolled her eyes, clearly uncomfortable with the compliment.

"It's getting late. We should go."

"How long are you here?" asked Elizabeth.

"Two more days. Then we must go to Montreal."

"Can you come to lunch tomorrow?"

"We'd be delighted." Marie-Josée got up. "I'm glad Peter talked me into coming." She headed for the door. Peter remained behind, while the others walked out of the house and down the driveway to say goodnight. Chloé and Marie-Josée got into their car, started it, and backed out. Elizabeth and Benedict waved goodbye then returned, holding hands. Peter wondered whether he'd ever seen them do this before.

"Well," said Benedict. "Elizabeth always wanted a daughter. This is the next best thing."

"We can visit her in France. Goodness, this has been quite a day. I think I'm going to bed now." Elizabeth came over and kissed Peter, this time on the mouth. "Thank you."

After Elizabeth had gone upstairs, Benedict offered Peter a brandy.

"I can't drink brandy anymore. I might manage a Cointreau."

Benedict poured him a generous shot.

"Remarkable woman, Marie-Josée," Peter said. "No wonder Alastair couldn't resist her."

"Alastair couldn't resist anything."

"Marie-Josée thought you blamed her. She thought you were hostile to her."

"It was Alastair we were hostile to. And he to us. Especially Elizabeth. I suppose Elizabeth did blame Marie-Josée."

"She'll forgive her now?"

"Elizabeth is very positive about anyone who cares about children. Marie-Josée didn't have to take the girl on. She has children of her own, doesn't she?"

"Four, I think."

"A new interest. Just what we need."

Benedict lumbered up the stairs to bed, leaving Peter to finish his Cointreau. Peter stood and walked to the window. Above the tangled garden the moon was shining. For a moment, it looked just like the moon above the terrace of the hotel in Siem Reap. The memory of the laughter of the young lovers echoed in his ears. They had been reckless. Alastair had paid the price. But Marie-Josée had gone on, a force of nature.

ACKNOWLEDGEMENTS

I HAVE BEEN WRITING all my life beginning with a play that I co-wrote with my friend Dick Williams in Grade One, entitled "Cat and Dog." This masterpiece has unfortunately been lost. However I continued to scribble away through my teens and early twenties, mainly in the form of plays. Some of these stories began to take shape in pieces that I wrote in my late twenties. They have been considerably revised but reflect my observations and experiences over the past fifty years. I am extremely grateful to my editor Marc Côté who helped me to refine and polish them.

The cover artwork is from a painting by Barker Fairley and is reproduced here by kind permission of his estate and the Arts and Letters Club of Toronto where it hangs in the LAMPS room.